MONTANA MAVERICKS

Welcome to Big Sky Country! Where spirited men and women discover love on the range.

MONTANA MAVERICKS: BEHIND CLOSED DOORS

Shh! Can you keep a secret? The mayor has resigned and the town is in a tizzy. From fake romances to clandestine crushes, nothing in Tenacity is as it seems. The only thing these cowboys know for sure is this: They need the love of a good woman to make things right!

Under other circumstances, this would be the best day of Winter Hernandez's life. Unfortunately, Luca Sanchez is marrying Winter only to protect her from her ex and to give her child a name. He may have rescued her, but now her heart is in jeopardy. She has broken the rules of their agreement by falling for her convenient groom—and she doesn't dare let him know!

Dear Reader,

Recent divorcée Winter Hernandez came to Tenacity for a new start—not a new husband! But when she tells her old friend Luca Sanchez about her positive pregnancy test, the handsome cowboy immediately proposes marriage—to keep her ex-husband from claiming custody.

Five days later, Luca and Winter are husband and wife!

Of course, marriage is an adjustment for every couple—and especially a couple whose first kiss happened on the day of their engagment! But as the holidays grow closer, so, too, do the newlyweds.

Still, it's going to take some doing for the expectant bride to convince her convenient groom that she wants a *real* marriage. In the meantime, there's a Christmas tree to decorate, a holiday concert to enjoy, a Santa Claus parade to attend and a crooked mayor to confront.

Celebrating the holiday season with Luca and his family makes Winter feel as if she's truly found a home for herself and her unborn child—until the unexpected arrival of her ex threatens to destroy her newfound happiness.

I hope you enjoy Winter and Luca's story and all the other books in *Montana Mavericks: Behind Closed Doors*.

Happy Reading & Happy Holidays!

xo *Brenda*

THE MAVERICK'S MISTLETOE BRIDE

BRENDA HARLEN

Harlequin

MONTANA MAVERICKS

If you purchased this book without a cover you should be aware that this book is stolen property. It was reported as "unsold and destroyed" to the publisher, and neither the author nor the publisher has received any payment for this "stripped book."

MIX
Paper | Supporting responsible forestry
FSC® C021394

Special thanks and acknowledgment are given to Brenda Harlen for her contribution to the Montana Mavericks: Behind Closed Doors miniseries.

Harlequin
MONTANA MAVERICKS

ISBN-13: 978-1-335-54085-0

The Maverick's Mistletoe Bride

Copyright © 2025 by Harlequin Enterprises ULC

All rights reserved. No part of this book may be used or reproduced in any manner whatsoever without written permission.

Without limiting the author's and publisher's exclusive rights, any unauthorized use of this publication to train generative artificial intelligence (AI) technologies is expressly prohibited.

This is a work of fiction. Names, characters, places and incidents are either the product of the author's imagination or are used fictitiously. Any resemblance to actual persons, living or dead, businesses, companies, events or locales is entirely coincidental.

For questions and comments about the quality of this book, please contact us at CustomerService@Harlequin.com.

TM and ® are trademarks of Harlequin Enterprises ULC.

Harlequin Enterprises ULC
22 Adelaide St. West, 41st Floor
Toronto, Ontario M5H 4E3, Canada
www.Harlequin.com

HarperCollins Publishers
Macken House, 39/40 Mayor Street Upper,
Dublin 1, D01 C9W8, Ireland
www.HarperCollins.com

Printed in Lithuania

Brenda Harlen is a former attorney who once had the privilege of appearing before the Supreme Court of Canada. The practice of law taught her a lot about the world and reinforced her determination to become a writer—because in fiction, she could promise a happy ending! Now she is an award-winning, RITA® Award–nominated, nationally bestselling author of seventy titles for Harlequin. You can keep up-to-date with Brenda on Facebook and X, or through her website, brendaharlen.com.

Books by Brenda Harlen

Montana Mavericks: Behind Closed Doors

The Maverick's Mistletoe Bride

Montana Mavericks: The Trail to Tenacity

The Maverick's Resolution

Harlequin Special Edition

The Cowboys of Whispering Canyon

The Rancher's Temptation

Visit the Author Profile page
at Harlequin.com for more titles.

For Stephen Sundquist, fellow MAC alumni
and longtime friend, who willingly answers
random questions and shares his expertise—
and who's been waiting a long time for a dedication.
Thanks for everything! xo

Chapter One

Winter Hernandez's hands were shaking as she pulled the slender box out of her purse and tore it open, and she mentally chided herself for the display of nerves. There was no reason to be nervous. The only reason she'd picked up the test was to reassure herself that she wasn't pregnant. Because it was inconceivable that, three months after her divorce, she could be.

True, she'd been queasy, off and on, for several weeks now, but considering she'd recently uprooted herself from her home and her life in Butte—a necessary but nevertheless distressing event—she'd figured emotional upset was to blame. And if she'd also been uncharacteristically tired since she'd moved to Tenacity, she didn't think that was surprising, either. The past six months had been nothing but upheaval—starting with the announcement of her dad's promotion in June, followed by helping her parents pack up in anticipation of their relocation to Texas and then, when they were gone, finally forcing herself to face the truth she'd been unwilling to acknowledge for too long—that the man she'd married almost four years earlier wasn't the Prince Charming she'd once believed him to be.

She'd realized in October that her period was late, but she hadn't been concerned. Her cycle had always been erratic and easily affected by any kind of emotional upset or even a slight weight loss. Which was why she hadn't given it a second thought until she was skimming through her calendar earlier that morning and realized she hadn't had a period since she moved to Tenacity.

Now here she was, with pregnancy test in hand, to reassure herself that there was still no cause for concern.

She read the leaflet in the box twice, followed the directions exactly, then set the timer on her phone to await the results.

While she waited, one thought continued to echo in her mind like a fervent prayer: *Please let the test be negative.*

She wasn't prepared to have a baby at this stage in her life, with the ink barely dry on her divorce papers. More important, she didn't *ever* want to have Matt Hathaway's baby. She didn't want anything to tie her to the man she'd once imagined being with forever.

And if she was pregnant, she'd have much bigger worries than how that revelation would impact her life. A far greater concern was the well-being of an innocent child who would be helpless against its father's bullying. Which meant that there was only one course of action for Winter—to go somewhere far away where her ex-husband would never find her.

Please, please, please let the test be negative.

She jolted when the timer buzzed.

Heart pounding, stomach churning, she reached for the stick again, turning it over to look at the display window.

Oh God.

It was a good thing she was already sitting down, because her knees suddenly turned to jelly.

Pregnant

She stared at the single word for a long time, as if she might will the word "not" to appear in front of it.

Unfortunately, the result remained unchanged.

She was pregnant.

But that simple statement of fact failed to paint a complete picture of her current situation. She was twenty-eight years old, recently divorced, working part-time as a bookkeeper and sleeping on a pullout sofa in her cousin's basement—none of which suggested she was capable of taking care of a child on her own.

But that was exactly what she'd have to do. There was no other option.

She returned the stick to the box and dropped her face into her hands, her eyes burning and her throat tight.

Why was this happening?

Why now, when she'd finally started to take back control of her life?

Or maybe the belief that she was making progress toward re-establishing her autonomy was nothing more than an illusion. A tentative spark of hope quickly snuffed out by the reality of that single, unchanging word in the display window.

Pregnant

But how had it happened?

She wasn't wondering about the logistics of reproduction, obviously, but about how it had happened to her—because she'd gone on birth control several weeks before her wedding.

When Matt had first slid the diamond ring on her finger, she'd looked forward to all the traditional milestones of marriage with giddy anticipation. She'd dreamed of the day they'd exchange vows, move into their first home together and, of course, have his baby—hopefully even several babies. But while Matt had talked eagerly, even at the very beginning, about growing their family, Winter hadn't been ready just yet. Of course she wanted to be a mother someday—but not nine months after their wedding.

And definitely not six months after the dissolution of their marriage.

Aside from the fact that the timing couldn't be worse, she really didn't understand how it happened when she'd always been diligent about taking her birth control pills. *Always.*

Until her pills ran out, she remembered now.

She'd been due to see her doctor for a prescription renewal

at the end of the summer, but by then, she'd known that her marriage was over and all that was left was to serve Matt with the papers.

Despite his unwillingness to talk about divorce, it was apparent to Winter that he'd already lost interest in her as they hadn't shared a bed in months, and she'd resolved to pack up and move out when he was out of town on his next business trip. But the Saturday before that trip, he came home after poker night with his buddies and climbed into bed with her.

She'd been surprised when he kissed her—and also wary. She knew that if she turned away or asked him to leave, it would cause a big scene and she was tired of the scenes. Also, she suspected that causing a scene wouldn't prevent him from taking what he wanted, because he liked to remind her that he had husbandly rights and she had wifely duties.

So she didn't turn away and she didn't ask him to leave, and one thing had led to another. And perhaps, in her own way, she was saying goodbye to her husband, because she knew it was the last time they would be together.

When he returned from his business trip three days later, she was already gone but a process server was waiting to serve him with her petition for divorce.

She didn't know if he tried to call her when he got the papers, because she'd changed her number before she left Butte. But she did know that he never bothered to file a response, because three weeks later, her divorce was finalized.

Now she was pregnant, and if Matt found out, she'd be trapped forever—the termination of their marriage notwithstanding. And that was why he could never find out.

Luca had finished pitching the last of the hay on top of the fresh snow for the hungry cattle when his phone vibrated in his pocket. He dropped the pitchfork into the bed of the pickup and pulled out the cell, then yanked off his glove to open the screen and read the message. He tapped a quick reply—or as quick as he could manage with fingers numb from the cold—and tucked it away again before hopping into the passenger seat of the cab.

Dusty, another of the hands that he frequently worked with at Cedar Ridge Ranch, was behind the wheel, his phone pressed to his ear, murmuring softly. Luca had done most of the hard labor this morning while Dusty attempted to placate his wife, who'd had the locks changed on their house when she heard he'd been spotted at an out-of-town strip club.

"I'll be home right after work today, I promise," Dusty said now.

Luca rubbed his hands on his thighs, attempting to restore circulation to his frozen digits.

"It's a cold one out there today," Dusty remarked, when he'd finally ended his call.

"Says the guy who's been sitting in the toasty warm truck," Luca noted dryly.

The other man shifted the truck into gear. "Believe me, it would have been even colder at my house tonight if I hadn't managed to smooth things over with Mindy."

"You wouldn't have had to smooth things over if you hadn't stayed out until 2:00 a.m."

"I was with my brother, celebrating his birthday."

"At a strip club?"

"At a gentleman's club," Dusty said indignantly.

Luca snorted.

"And anyway, it's not like I've got any reason to want to be home. Since the baby was born, he sees a lot more of Mindy's boobs than I do."

"Considering that baby is your son, you might try to be a little more tolerant and understanding."

"I figured giving her space was the best way to show my tolerance and understanding."

"And how did that work out for you?" Luca asked.

"Not as well as I'd hoped," the other man admitted.

Luca hopped out of the truck again when Dusty paused at the fence, unlatching the gate and swinging it wide so the other man could drive through, then closing it behind the vehicle again to keep the cattle secured.

"Now that the cows are fed, maybe we can break for lunch," Luca suggested, when he was back in the truck and Dusty continued toward the barn.

"It's not even eleven o'clock."

"And we've been at it since six," Luca pointed out.

"I've never known anyone to be in such a hurry for tuna melts."

"Actually, I'm going to head into town for lunch today."

"Castillo's?" Dusty guessed, with a telltale smirk that said he suspected Luca's plans were more likely linked to a specific woman who worked at the restaurant rather than the food served there.

"Can't beat their enchiladas," Luca said.

"Yeah, cuz we all know you drive into town for enchiladas."

"I've got some errands to run after lunch, too, so I might be a while."

"Errands, huh?" Dusty snorted. "Is that what kids are calling it these days?"

"Can you cover for me if I'm late?" Luca asked, choosing to ignore the other man's question.

"Why should I?"

"Maybe because I did my job and yours this morning?" Luca suggested.

"Yeah. Okay," Dusty said, a grudging acknowledgment of the fact.

It wasn't a long drive from the ranch to Castillo's, where Winter worked part-time as a bookkeeper, and Luca managed to shave several minutes off the journey by exceeding the speed limit a little. Though her text message had been both brief and vague—Any chance you could pick me up at work?—he'd sensed a degree of urgency in her request.

And so he'd responded:

Be there asap.

Or maybe his sister Nina was right and Luca had a white knight complex that compelled him to offer assistance to a damsel in distress—even if that distress existed only in his imagination.

But he couldn't deny that he felt as protective of Winter as he did of his sisters. Perhaps because she was of a similar age and had gone to school with both of them. Growing up in a town with a modest population meant that there were rarely enough students in one grade to fill a classroom, resulting in most of them hosting split grades. When Winter found herself in the lower grade of a split, she would be in a class with Nina, who was a year older; when she was in the higher grade, she'd be a classmate of Marisa, who was a year younger. As a result, she'd become good friends with both of them, though they'd mostly lost touch with her, too, when her family moved to Butte shortly after her high school graduation.

Luca also couldn't deny that, since her return to Tenacity a few months earlier, he sometimes felt a stirring that was distinctly unfraternal when he was around Winter Hernandez—as she was now known again, having opted to take back her maiden name when she separated from her husband. A smart decision, in his opinion. Not just the name change but ditching Matt Hathaway, who'd given Luca all kinds of bad vibes when he'd met the man.

Despite the frigid temperature of this late November day, Winter was waiting outside the restaurant when Luca pulled up in front. She was appropriately attired for the weather, in a puffy coat, knitted hat and mittens, and winter boots, but still, the fact that she was standing in the cold rather than the cozy interior confirmed his suspicion that something was wrong. Before he had a chance to hop out and go around to open her door, she was climbing into the passenger seat.

"Hey," he said, as she pulled the seat belt across her body and secured the buckle.

She tried to smile, but her lips trembled rather than curved, and her voice was quiet, uncertain, when she replied, "Thanks for coming."

He'd noted her subdued demeanor when their paths had crossed at the Pumpkin Spice Crawl several weeks back and had wondered then if it was a reflection of maturity or a souvenir of her failed marriage. Either way, he'd found himself missing the vibrant, confident young woman he remembered.

Since then, he'd caught occasional glimpses of her former self in a happy smile or—even more rarely—a spontaneous laugh. But there was no hint of a smile or laugh now.

"Anytime," he said.

It was a simple but sincere reply, so he was a little taken aback when Winter responded to it by starting to cry.

"Hey," he said again, more gently this time. "Whatever's going on, surely it can't be all that bad."

"You're right. It's not all that bad." She tugged off her hat and mittens and stacked them neatly in her lap. "It's worse."

"You want to talk about it?" he asked.

She shook her head. "Not here."

Which was when he realized he was still parked outside the doors of the restaurant.

"Okay," he agreed, pulling away from the curb. "Where do you want to go?"

She nibbled on her lower lip as she mulled over the question for a minute. "Can we go to your place?" she finally asked.

"I live with my parents," he felt compelled to point out.

A few years earlier, he'd started looking for a place of his own, simply because he'd decided that a man closing in on his thirtieth birthday shouldn't be living with his mom and dad. But there weren't a lot of rentals available in Tenacity, and fewer still within his price range and a reasonable commute to work, so he'd abandoned his search only a few weeks later. And while the living quarters had been tight with Julian, Diego, Nina and Marisa still at home, too, they'd managed. And over the past couple of years, as his siblings had, one by one, gotten engaged or married and moved out, he'd decided that he was content enough right where he was.

"Are they home?" Winter asked him now.

He shook his head. "They're both at work today."

"Which is where you should be, too," she said. "I'm sorry. I shouldn't have reached out to you."

"I'm glad you did," he replied.

"I don't know why I did," she confided. "I don't know why I thought you could help. And then—" her breath hitched "—you didn't even hesitate. You just showed up…because I asked."

"Did you want me not to show up?" he asked lightly.

She shook her head. "No. But I wonder why you did. Why you would. Why I'd message you—and somehow know that you would."

"Maybe because friends are there for one another," he suggested.

She scrubbed her tearstained cheeks with the palms of her hands. "Thank you, friend."

"You're welcome."

Twenty minutes later, Luca pulled into the drive leading to the bungalow that his parents rented on Cedar Ridge Ranch and that had been their home for longer than he'd been alive.

His family history was a simple and familiar one. His paternal grandparents—Miguel and Liliana Sanchez—had emigrated from Mexico shortly after they married, wanting to make a better life for themselves and their children in America. Miguel had a knack with horses and quickly found work on a cattle ranch in Tenacity, Montana, and Liliana was hired to cook for the ranch hands.

When their sons were old enough to follow their own paths, Aaron chose one that led him to Bronco, Montana, where he got a job with the post office and married Denise, who worked in a hair salon. But Will only ever aspired to work the land as his father had done, and he remained in Tenacity doing just that, eventually marrying Nicole, another Mexican American, who helped support the family by tending their vegetable garden and working as a seamstress.

Luca was the youngest son and the middle of their five children, and if at times it had felt cramped in their modest three-bedroom home, he'd been taught to appreciate what he had—a roof over his head, food on the table and family all around. And while money was often tight, there was never any shortage of love and affection in their home.

He parked his truck in front of that home now and got out. This time, Winter waited for him to come around to her door—or maybe she remained immobile because she'd changed her mind about being here.

"It'll be warmer inside," he promised, when she made no move to get out of the truck.

"Are you sure this is okay?" she asked.

"I'm thirty-one years old," he noted dryly. "I don't need my parents' permission to have a friend over."

She managed a small smile as she unclipped her belt and slid out of the seat.

"Careful," he said, taking her arm to guide her up the walk. "It might be slippery."

She nodded.

He unlocked the door and pushed it open, urging Winter over the threshold ahead of him.

"Déjà vu," she murmured softly, as she stepped inside.

"Does it look exactly as you remember?"

"Not exactly," she said. "But it feels the same. Warm and welcoming. No wonder I always loved hanging out here with Nina and Marisa."

"My mom would be pleased to hear that."

"She used to work from home," Winter recalled.

"She still does most of the time," Luca confided. "But on Mondays, there's a clothing swap at the church. She helps out with the exchange and does alterations and minor fixes, as required."

"Why am I not surprised?" she asked, just a hint of a smile curving her lips.

But somehow that hint was enough to stir the uncomfortable feeling that he was reluctant to acknowledge as physical attraction. Because she was Winter Hernandez—the girl who'd gone to school with his sisters.

Except that she wasn't a girl anymore. Though the top of her head didn't come to his chin, her feminine curves attested to the fact that she was a woman now—and a stunningly beautiful one at that, with silky dark hair that fell to the middle of her back and big brown eyes fringed with long, thick lashes, a pert little nose with a sprinkling of freckles and a lush, kissable mouth.

He took a deliberate step away from her, away from that kissable mouth, and refocused on the topic of their conversation. "It was often a struggle for my parents, raising five kids on a minimal income, but they taught us to be grateful for what we had and showed us that there are always ways to help those who had less."

"Your parents are really good people," Winter said, as they removed their coats and boots. "Which is probably why you and your siblings grew up to be really good people."

"We were fortunate to be raised in a house filled with love," he acknowledged. "Even if the pantry was sometimes empty."

"I imagine it was hard to keep it filled with five hungry kids," she noted. "Though I seem to recall that there were always homemade cookies in the cookie jar."

"I'll bet that's true even now, if you want to take a look," he offered, leading the way to the kitchen.

"Thanks, but I'll pass," she said.

"How about something to drink?" he suggested as an alternative. "Coffee? Tea? Hot cocoa?"

She'd started to shake her head, then paused, reconsidering. "Actually, hot cocoa sounds good."

"Coming right up," he promised.

She settled herself at the table and watched while he gathered the necessary equipment and ingredients. He poured milk into a saucepan and set it on the stove, then measured cocoa powder and sugar.

"When you offered hot cocoa, I thought you'd boil the kettle and tear open an envelope of instant mix."

"Never," he said, sounding scandalized.

"It's what you'd get at my place, if I offered you hot cocoa."

"And why I know now to never accept your offer of hot cocoa."

"It's really not that bad," she told him.

"I've had prepackaged hot cocoa," he said. "It's not that good, either."

When steam began to rise from the milk, he whisked in cocoa powder and sugar. Then he tossed in a handful of chocolate chips and continued to whisk.

"I'm never going to be satisfied with prepackaged hot cocoa again, am I?" she mused.

"As long as I don't leave you dissatisfied, my work is done."

He intended the words as a playful retort, but as soon as they were out of his mouth, he wished he could take them back.

But of course he couldn't, and they seemed to hang in the air between them for a long, achingly awkward moment.

Winter recovered first and responded lightly, "I can't imagine that you've ever had any complaints."

"No," he agreed, grateful that she hadn't been offended by his remark. "No complaints."

"About your hot cocoa?" she prompted.

He grinned. "Not about that, either."

She surprised him again by laughing, though he noticed that warm color had suffused her cheeks.

He turned away to remove the saucepan from the burner, then added a splash of half-and-half and a few drops of vanilla extract. After dividing the steaming liquid between two large mugs, he topped each with a handful of miniature marshmallows.

"I'm seriously impressed," Winter said, when he set one of the mugs in front of her. "And wondering how it is that a man who can make hot cocoa like this hasn't been caught by some lucky woman."

"I'm slippery," he said with a wink. "Like a greased pig."

She made a face at that. "I've never understood why anyone would want to grease a pig."

He shrugged. "For fun? For sport?"

"I'll take your word for it."

Luca took another sip of his cocoa before he asked, "Are you ready to talk about it now?"

Winter sighed, her gaze focused on the contents of her mug. "I've made such a mess of everything."

"Messes can be cleaned up," he assured her.

"Not this one," she said.

"Tell me," he urged.

"I think… I'm going to have to leave Tenacity."

He waited for an explanation, and when none was immediately forthcoming, he asked, "Did you rob a bank? Kill a man?"

"No," she said. "Obviously."

"Streak naked down Main Street?"

"Again, no."

"Have a fight with your cousin?"

She shook her head. "Rafael and Sera have been nothing but wonderful since I showed up at their door three months ago."

"Something happened today?" he guessed.

Now she nodded. "I got some...unexpected news."

"What kind of unexpected news?"

She reached into her purse and pulled out a plastic stick.

Not just a plastic stick, he realized. A pregnancy test.

A *positive* pregnancy test.

Chapter Two

Luca might have been less surprised if she'd confessed to running naked through town, because so far as he knew, Winter hadn't dated anyone since she'd separated from her husband. And while he'd recently found himself wondering if she might be willing to go out with him, when she was ready to start dating again, this unexpected news effectively put a kibosh on that plan.

"I'm not sure what to say," he admitted. "Congratulations?"

Her eyes welled with fresh tears. "Thanks."

"Have you told the baby's father?"

She shook her head. "I took the test less than an hour ago. The only person I've told is you."

"But you are going to have the baby?" he asked.

"Of course, I'm going to have the baby." Her tone assured him there was no question about that.

"Okay," he said. "But there are options, if you're not one hundred percent certain."

"There aren't any options for me—I'm almost sixteen weeks into my pregnancy."

His brows lifted at that.

"I know," she said. "I feel like such a fool."

"You're hardly the first woman to have an unplanned pregnancy."

"It's not just that this was unplanned, but that I didn't even suspect that I might be pregnant until this morning—when I realized I hadn't had a period since before I moved in with Rafael and Sera."

"So...it's Matt's baby?"

"Of course, it's Matt's baby. Did you really think I'd been with someone else in the short time that I've been divorced?"

"No," he said, not sure if he was more relieved that she hadn't hooked up with some other guy or worried that she was having her ex-husband's baby.

Not that he knew Matt Hathaway well—in fact, he'd only met him once. But that one time had been enough to assure Luca that the other man wouldn't willingly give up what was his, and it had been obvious that the man considered Winter to be his.

"And now that you know you're pregnant—does it change your feelings for Matt?" Luca asked cautiously.

She answered firmly and without hesitation. "No."

He exhaled a silent sigh of relief. Still, he felt compelled to ask, "You don't wish you were still married to the father of your baby?"

"No." This time she emphasized her response with a shake of her head. "And that's why I have to leave Tenacity. I have to go somewhere Matt will never find me—so he can never find my baby.

"Maybe you think that's harsh," she continued, when he didn't respond. "That he has parental rights, but he gave up any rights to be a father to my baby when he..." Her eyes filled with tears again as her words trailed off. "He gave up his rights."

"Okay," Luca agreed, not wanting to cause her any more distress. Obviously there were reasons she'd petitioned for divorce—reasons she wasn't ready to talk about—and though his protective instincts reared up again, he didn't think she'd appreciate him tracking down her ex-husband to extract payback for whatever those reasons might be.

"Tell me what you need me to do," he said instead. "How can I help?"

"I don't know," she admitted. "Obviously I didn't take any time to think this through. When I saw the word *pregnant* on the test stick, I panicked. I needed some time and space to think. To figure out what I'm going to do."

"Do you want me to leave you alone—to give you that time and space?"

She shook her head. "No. I know what I need to do now. I need to leave Tenacity."

Luca wasn't keen on that idea—or the determination in her tone—but he also knew better than to attempt to tell her what to do.

Instead, he asked cautiously, "Where would you go?"

She sighed. "That I don't know."

"Texas?"

"That was my first instinct," she confided. "And the first place that Matt would look for me."

"Surely your parents would want to help you—and their grandchild."

"You'd think so," she agreed. "But my mom still hasn't forgiven me for leaving Matt and I suspect she would push me to reconcile, for the sake of our baby."

"They must realize you had reasons for ending your marriage."

"I didn't share many details," she admitted.

"Why not?"

"Because I was afraid they wouldn't believe me," she told him. "Because Matt was never anything but charming and solicitous around other people—and especially with my parents."

"I can't say that I found him particularly charming or solicitous," Luca remarked.

"You caught him in an unguarded moment. Or maybe he was caught off guard when he saw us together."

"I'd say he was jealous," he noted, recalling the hard anger of the other man's face when Matt saw his wife with her old friend.

She hesitated a second, then nodded. "Jealous, possessive, controlling."

"Abusive?" he asked through gritted teeth.

She responded with another short nod. "Mostly it was emotional and verbal abuse."

"Which is still abuse."

"You're right," she acknowledged. "But it's a lot harder to prove, because the bruises and scars aren't visible."

"You said *mostly* it was emotional and verbal abuse," he noted.

"I don't want to talk about my ex-husband anymore."

He backed off, wanting to assure her that he was a man who respected a woman's boundaries, but questions lingered in his mind and tangled in his gut.

"Suffice it to say, going to Texas isn't an option," she told him.

"So you know where you won't go, but you have yet to figure out where you will go," Luca said.

"Maybe upstate New York," she decided.

His brows rose. "Any particular reason?"

"I have a friend there," she confided. "Bethany was in several of the same classes in college, and we've kept in touch."

"Would you stay with her?"

"Not likely," she admitted. "She and her husband have a two-bedroom house and two kids under the age of three. But I'm sure she could help me find a place of my own."

"What about a job?" he asked.

"Obviously something else I'd have to find."

Now Luca frowned. "Why would you want to move more than two thousand miles across the country without having a place to stay or work to do?"

"Because I don't have a lot of other options."

"Doesn't it make sense to have something at least resembling a plan before you take off?"

"Of course, it makes sense," she snapped. "But apparently I'm incapable of making sense right now. I'm panicking and responding emotionally rather than rationally, which might explain why I called you."

"Okay, then," he said, obviously taken aback by her outburst.

She dropped her head into her hands. "I'm so sorry."

"No need to apologize," he assured her, though his tone was several degrees cooler than it had been previously.

"There is," she insisted. "And I *am* sorry. I'm just feeling... overwhelmed...and scared...and alone."

"You're not alone, Winter," he said, apparently already willing to forgive her. "And if you don't yet have a plan, then we'll come up with one."

"We?" she repeated, hating the desperate note in her voice.

"You called me because you wanted help, did you not?"

"I guess I did."

"So let me help."

"It would help if you took me back to Rafael and Sera's to pack and then drove me to the bus station."

"Staying here seems like a better option."

She looked around the bungalow. "That would be cozy, but I'm not sure your parents would approve."

"In Tenacity, I mean," he said, clarifying.

Now she shook her head. "Have you listened to anything I've said? I can't stay here, because Matt knows I have family here. And if he decides to look for me, this will be the second—or maybe third—place he looks."

Luca frowned at that. "If you think the first place is Texas, why would Tenacity be the third?"

"I might have asked a friend to tell him that I was heading to California," she confided.

"If you're that afraid of him—"

"I'm not afraid for me," she said. "Not anymore. But I am afraid for my baby."

Before he could respond to that, he heard boots stomping on the mat by the back door.

"Luca?" Nicole Sanchez called out, obviously surprised to find her son home in the middle of the day.

"In the kitchen," he replied.

His mom shrugged out of her coat as she came through the mud room, then paused, a smile lighting her face, when she saw his guest seated across from him at the table.

"Winter," Nicole said, moving to embrace the young woman who had risen to her feet. "What a wonderful surprise it is to see you."

"It's wonderful to see you, too, Mrs. Sanchez," she said, hugging her back.

His mom chuckled. "I think you can probably call me Nicole now."

"Probably not," Winter said, with a small smile and a half shrug. "Old habits."

"Well, if we're going to be seeing more of you—and I hope we are—then I want you to at least consider dropping the formalities."

"I'll try."

"Can you stay for dinner tonight?"

"Thank you for the offer, but no, I can't." She glanced at her watch. "In fact, I'm already late getting back to work."

"I need to get back, too," Luca said, pushing his chair away from the table. Then he dropped a kiss on his mom's cheek. "But I will be home for dinner."

"Then I guess I better decide what I'm cooking," she mused.

"It's Monday," he reminded her. "My night to cook."

"Even better," Nicole said.

"So much for not being interrupted," Winter mused, when they were in Luca's truck and headed to town again.

"At least we were only sharing hot cocoa and conversation," he noted. "Not making out on the sofa."

"Did that happen a lot when you were a teenager—getting caught in a compromising position with a girl?" she asked curiously.

"Nope," he denied. "Once was enough."

She managed to smile at that, though he could tell she was still preoccupied with her own thoughts.

Her pregnancy.

He could only imagine how she'd felt when she saw the result of her test. No doubt she'd experienced a range of conflicting emotions, though he suspected panic was at the top of the list. And how had she responded? She'd reached out to him.

Luca was humbled by this demonstration of her trust in him—and determined to prove it hadn't been misplaced. Which meant that he needed to help her set a course of action that would ensure the safety of Winter and her unborn child.

It might have helped to have more specifics about how and why her marriage had ended, but despite her reluctance to share details, she'd provided enough information for him to know that she was afraid of her husband. And that knowledge made Luca want to track down Matt Hathaway and give him reason to feel fear.

"Is it really your turn to cook dinner tonight?"

Winter's question interrupted his meandering thoughts and drew Luca back to the present.

He nodded. "Mondays and Fridays. Though I sometimes cheat on Fridays and pick up pizza."

"In the almost four years I was married, Matt never once offered to cook a meal," she said. "He'd throw steaks or burgers or ribs on the grill, if I asked, but he never took the initiative to plan and prepare a meal.

"Not that I expected him to," she admitted. "Because I grew

up in a traditional home with a mom who was the stereotypical housewife, responsible for all the domestic chores."

"You were also an only child," Luca pointed out. "So your mom was only taking care of a husband and one kid—mine had five and decided early on that we all needed to pull our weight."

"Kudos to her."

"She also claimed that knowing how to cook and clean for ourselves would make us more marriageable and, considering that each of my siblings is now paired off, there might be some truth to her argument."

"Everyone except you," Winter mused. "Obviously she didn't count on you being so slippery."

He chuckled. "She seems content to let me take my time to settle down—at least since my brothers and sisters have kept her busy planning their weddings."

"I remember Barrett Deroy from way back when," Winter said now. "So I was happy to hear that he and Nina found their way back to one another. And I met Marisa's husband last week, when they came into Castillo's for lunch. He seems like a good guy, too."

"Dawson is that," Luca confirmed. "And they're blissfully happy together."

"How long have they been married?"

He had to think about that for a minute. "Since the beginning of February so...ten months, I guess."

"Hopefully with every day that passes, he continues to prove that he really is the wonderful man she married."

"Unlike your husband, you mean?"

"*Ex*-husband," Winter reminded him. "But yes."

"You told me that he didn't contest the divorce," Luca recalled. "So isn't it possible that he's already moved on? That he might not have any interest in being a father to your baby?"

"The one thing I learned about Matt during the course of our marriage is that he's all about control," Winter told him now. "I moved out of our apartment when he was away on a business trip, because I knew he'd never let me go. Not because he loved me, but because I was his wife—which, in his mind, meant that I owed him deference and obedience. He would have been furious to return home and find I was gone, but at that point, there really wasn't anything he could do about it—aside from pleading his case to my mother."

"Did he do that?"

She nodded. "That's likely why she still hasn't forgiven me for ending the marriage. To Josefina, marriage is a sacred covenant and there's no justification for breaking it. And if she finds out I'm having Matt's baby…" Winter shook her head as her words trailed off. "She can't find out. She'll claim it's a sign from God that I should go back to my husband."

"You don't always have to do what your mother tells you," he pointed out gently.

"I know that. But I also know that she'll tell Matt about the baby, and he'll use our child to punish me. Oh, he'll play it like he's being benevolent and forgiving, offering to take me back so that our child can grow up with a mom and dad, and when I refuse, he'll go after custody—sole custody, of course, so that he can cut me out of the baby's life as much as possible."

"I can't imagine any court taking your baby away from you."

"It wouldn't happen right away," she acknowledged. "No doubt he'd wait to file for custody—an infant can be disruptive and demanding—but he'd make sure I knew that was his plan, so the threat would hang like a cloud over every day of our lives until it finally happened.

"And then he'd have his friends and colleagues write letters to the judge saying what a great guy and wonderful father he is, because he'd only ever let them see that side of him."

She turned her head to look at the window—maybe so he wouldn't see the unshed tears that glistened in her eyes.

"I'm the only one who knows what goes on behind closed

doors," she said softly. "And no one would believe me if I told them."

"I would. I do," Luca told her.

She managed a small smile. "Unfortunately, you're not a family court judge." Her smile faded then, her expression turning bleak. "Matt has an uncle who's a judge in Butte. Civil, I think, but no doubt he's got friends in other courts."

"Couldn't you file for custody here?"

"He'd argue that Butte is the proper jurisdiction because it's where we lived, where our baby was conceived, and that I moved away without his knowledge or consent."

No wonder she seemed so disheartened.

"And that's why I have to leave Tenacity now," she told him. "Before he—or anyone else—finds out about the baby. Because even worse than losing custody would be watching him destroy the child's spirit, which he could manage with nothing more than weekly visits."

"What if you got a restraining order?"

"Now? Four months after I walked out on our marriage?" She shook her head. "He'd argue that I was making unfounded accusations to undermine his future petition for custody. And aside from the unfounded part, he wouldn't be wrong."

"There has to be another way," Luca insisted.

"If you have a better idea, I'd be happy to hear it."

Unfortunately, at the moment, his mind was blank.

"Give me twenty-four hours," he urged instead.

"Nothing is going to change in twenty-four hours."

"Just promise me you won't make any final decisions until tomorrow—until we've had a chance to talk again. Please."

"Okay," she said, relenting. "Thank you."

"I'm not sure what you're thanking me for," he admitted.

"You listened to me," she said. "And it's been a long time since I've felt listened to."

* * *

Winter wasn't sure why she agreed to the twenty-four hours.

Maybe it was the *please* Luca had tacked onto the end of his request.

Maybe it was the fact that it was a request rather than an order or a demand.

Maybe it was that she'd always had a little bit of a crush on Luca—though she would have died of embarrassment if either of Nina or Marisa had ever suspected as much—and still had a soft spot in her heart that made it hard to say *no* to him.

Whatever the reason, she decided that spending one more day in Tenacity wouldn't make much of a difference, aside from allowing her to fine-tune the details of her plan, look at the job listings in Saratoga Springs and reach out to Bethany.

But aware of her imminent departure, she found herself lingering over dinner with Rafael and Sera and their kids—six-year-old Nicolas, four-year old Gabriel and Elena, twenty-two months—trying not to think about how much she'd miss the family connection when she was gone.

"Everything okay?" Sera asked, as they tidied up the kitchen together after the meal.

"Yeah." She forced a smile. "Why?"

"You just seem a little…sad tonight."

"Just thinking about my next steps," she said.

"What do you mean?"

"I've been here three months already. That's a long time to impose."

"Having you here has been a pleasure not an imposition," Sera assured her. "Though I can understand that you might want something more comfortable than a pullout sofa in the basement, which is why Rafael and I have been talking about getting a real bed for downstairs. And, when he manages to carve out some free time, he's going to put up walls so you'll have a proper bedroom."

"That's incredibly generous," Winter said, her throat tight. "But I can't live with you forever."

"Of course not," her cousin's wife agreed. "Just long enough to get your feet back under you."

"My feet are under me, and—"

Her response was interrupted by a knock on the door.

"I've got it," Rafael said, coming through the kitchen with Gabriel in a fireman's carry over his shoulder.

The four-year-old was giggling.

"Don't get him all wound up before bed," Sera admonished, but he was already gone.

"It's hard sometimes, managing baths and bedtime routines for three kids when Rafael's bartending," she said to Winter. "And sometimes even harder when he's home."

"I can understand that," she acknowledged.

"Which is only one of the reasons I've enjoyed having you here."

"Spending time with you and the kids is only one of the reasons I've enjoyed being here," Winter said. "But—"

Once again she was interrupted before she could finish her thought, this time by Rafael's return, Gabriel still over his shoulder, and Luca following on his heels.

"Winter's got a visitor," Rafael said, his brows raised in silent question. "*Un visitante masculino.*"

"Luca," she said.

"*¡Hola!*" He shifted his attention to Sera then. "I apologize for dropping by uninvited, but I was hoping to finish a conversation that Winter and I were having earlier."

"*No es un problema,*" Sera assured him, even as she looked to her husband's cousin for confirmation.

"I thought we were going to talk tomorrow," Winter said cautiously.

"I didn't want to wait until tomorrow," Luca told her.

Sera nudged her husband. "We should give them some privacy."

"If we give them privacy, how will we know what they're talking about?" Rafael asked.

"Maybe we should go for a drive," Luca suggested to Winter. She nodded.

"Don't be too late," Rafael cautioned. "It's a school night."

"I graduated a long time ago," Winter reminded her cousin.

"Yeah, but the kids will be stomping around early before they head off to school in the morning," he pointed out.

"I'll keep that in mind."

She didn't say anything else until they'd exited the house, and Luca was silent, too.

"So what's on your mind that couldn't wait until tomorrow?" she asked, when he was pulling out of her cousin's driveway.

"I was thinking about your reasons for coming to Tenacity—the fact that you have history and family here."

"Which is why Matt will look for me here," she reminded him.

"And you want to leave Tenacity because you're afraid that he'll seek custody of—or at least visitation with—your baby," he noted.

She nodded.

"I don't know much about family law—or any kind of law," he confided. "But Julian's wife's best friend is an experienced family law attorney, so after I left you today, I went to see Lynda Slater and asked some questions."

She frowned. "You told her about my situation?"

"I didn't give any names and I kept the details vague," he assured her.

"Okay," she said. "And what did you learn?"

"The simplest way to negate your ex-husband's parental rights would be for another man to claim paternity, and the simplest way for another man to claim paternity would be to marry him."

"None of that seems simple to me," she told him. "Aside from the fact that I'm not eager to jump into marriage again, there's no way I could trick someone else into marrying me and then claim he's the father of a baby that would be born only five months after the wedding—and that's assuming he'd want to get married right away."

"I'm not suggesting you trick anyone," Luca argued. "I'm suggesting you marry me."

Chapter Three

Winter stared at Luca, stunned.

Her childhood crush had just asked her to marry him, and she didn't know whether to laugh or cry.

Not that it had been the proposal of her dreams—and it was unlikely that of any other woman's dreams, either. He hadn't gotten down on one knee with a ring in hand, and he hadn't issued any declarations of love or made promises about happily-ever-after. Instead, he'd simply suggested marriage as a solution to her current dilemma.

And still, despite the absence of romantic gestures or loving vows, she was more than a little tempted to accept his impulsive offer—to seize the opportunity to realize her secret teenage dream of walking down the aisle in a white dress to exchange vows with Luca Sanchez.

But in that fantasy, she hadn't been pregnant with another man's baby.

"You can't be serious," she said, though there was a tiny part of her heart that wished he was not only serious but sincere—that this amazing man could actually want to marry her.

"Why not?" he challenged.

"Because."

"Because isn't an answer," he admonished.

"Because it's crazy," she told him.

"Not as crazy as you running off to God-only-knows-where to start your life over in an unfamiliar town where you don't have a place to live or a job to pay rent or anyone to help you take care of your baby."

"I realize it isn't an ideal scenario," she acknowledged, a little defensively. "But I need to start over with a clean slate."

"If I believed that leaving town was truly what you wanted, I'd help you in any way that I could," he told her. "But you don't want to leave—you feel that it's what you have to do."

"Because it *is* what I have to do."

"You promised to give me time to come up with another plan, and I did that."

"Marriage isn't a plan," she said. "It's…desperation."

"Isn't there a saying about desperate times calling for desperate measures?"

"*I'm* desperate," she acknowledged. "*You're* not."

"Before you reject my proposal out of hand, could you take a minute to think about it?"

"No," she said. "Because if I think about it, I'll say *yes*."

"Because you know it's the best solution."

"Because I'm desperate," she reminded him.

And what he was offering was quite possibly the answer to her prayers.

But what would Luca get out of it?

Why would he be willing to put his life on hold to marry her?

"I can't tell you how much it means to me that you'd be willing to go to such lengths to help me out," she told him sincerely. "But this isn't your problem to solve, Luca."

"I'm not offering to solve a problem," he told her. "I'm offering you the chance to give your baby the security and stability of being born to a mom and a dad who will love him or her—with lots of other family members hovering in the background, offering advice and support and occasional babysitting services."

He was painting a tempting picture, and she was undeniably tempted, but she shook her head. "It won't work."

"Why not?"

"Because no one is going to believe that my baby is yours."

"They will if we tell them it is."

"Are you really willing to lie to your friends and neighbors—and even your family—for me?"

"I am if it will keep you here in Tenacity, close to your family and friends, where I won't have to worry about you, pregnant and alone and on the run."

"You don't have to worry about me," she told him. "I'm not your responsibility."

"But I will worry—because I care about you."

The words were simple but sincere, and her eyes filled again.

"I'm sorry," she said, swiping at the tears that spilled over.

"Why are you apologizing?" he asked gently.

"Because I'm not usually such a crybaby." She sniffled. "I think it's the pregnancy hormones."

"No doubt that's part of it," he acknowledged, dabbing at the streaks of moisture on her cheeks with a handkerchief he pulled from his pocket. "Another part might be that you're feeling overwhelmed because you don't have a plan for your future, which is why I've presented you with one."

"Do you really think a wedding should be part of that plan?" she asked dubiously.

"I do," he said, then grinned as he realized his words were like wedding vows.

"You're really willing to marry me?"

"I wouldn't have suggested it if I wasn't prepared to go through with it."

"People will have questions," she warned.

"Then we better make sure we have answers."

"Okay," she said. "How and when did we…hook up?"

He considered for a minute. "When our paths crossed at the Pumpkin Spice Festival? Everyone saw us there together."

He was probably right about that, as almost everyone in town had been at the festival. And though she remembered the surprising feelings of happiness and warmth that filled her heart as she sat and chatted with Luca, how pleased she'd been to listen as he regaled her with the details of his unexpected discovery of dinosaur bones, she wasn't sure anyone who saw them together would believe romance had been in the air.

But that wasn't even the biggest obstacle, she realized, as she counted back to that day and shook her head. "That was only seven weeks ago. I'm already sixteen weeks pregnant."

"When did you start your job at Castillo's?"

"The beginning of September—right after I moved in with Rafael and Sera."

"And I came into the restaurant for lunch one day, our eyes met and sparks flew."

She was unconvinced. "The date of conception would still be off by a few weeks—and that's assuming I jumped into bed with you almost immediately."

"I do have that effect on women," he said, with a playful wink.

She rolled her eyes.

"And anyway, my mom's fond of saying that babies are born when they're ready to be born—and sometimes babies come early, as ours will do."

"And what if he or she actually does come early?" Winter asked worriedly.

"Why don't we focus on the things we can control rather than worry about the things we can't?" he suggested.

"Because I don't feel as if anything's in my control right now," she admitted.

"Our story is ours to tell—and I'm sure plenty of people saw us together at the festival, lending validity to the claim that we'd already…reconnected."

"Plenty of those people also likely saw us go our separate ways."

"But driven by passion to meet up again later, away from prying eyes and loose lips."

Now she looked even more skeptical.

"Okay, it might take some effort to sell that," he acknowledged, reaching across the console for her hand.

Winter felt a jolt—an electrical current that reverberated from the point of contact through her whole body. She immediately pulled her hand back as her eyes flew to his, where she saw her own surprise reflected in the dark depths.

He cleared his throat. "And if we're going to sell it, you can't jump out of your skin every time I touch you."

"I'm sorry," she said.

"I don't want you to be sorry," he said. "I want you to be comfortable with me."

"I'm not *un*comfortable," she said. "I'm just a little…nervous."

"I'm not going to hurt you, Winter."

"I know."

"Do you?" he challenged.

She held his gaze, nodded. "I was fooled by Matt—charmed by his manners and seduced by his smile—because I didn't take the time to look beyond the surface. But I've known you for a long time, and I know I can trust you."

"That's a start," he said. "Now I've got a ring to put on your finger, if you'll let me, to make our engagement official."

"Okay," she said, and held out her left hand to him.

"Okay?" he echoed. "Could you maybe show a little more enthusiasm so that when people ask for the details of our engagement, we have a story to tell?"

"Maybe you should start with an actual proposal then, instead of just telling me you've got a ring to put on my finger," she suggested.

"Fair point," he acknowledged, taking her hand to link their fingers together. "Three months ago, when you came back to

Tenacity, I couldn't help but remember the girl that you'd been and, at the same time, yearn for the woman you'd become. Since then, I've never been happier than I am when I'm with you, so I'm asking you now, Winter Hernandez, will you marry me and spend every day of the rest of your life with me?"

"That was better," Winter said. "Much better." And her heart ached because she wished it was true and not just the setup for a story that they could tell other people.

"I'm still waiting for an answer," he pointed out.

"Yes, Luca Sanchez, I will marry you and look forward to every day of the rest of our lives together."

He took the ring—a modest diamond solitaire in a simple gold band that had been left to him on the passing of his paternal great-grandmother—and slid it on her third finger.

"It fits," she noted.

"Almost as if it was meant to be," he said lightly.

"Are you going to kiss me now?"

Luca nearly swallowed his tongue. "You want me to kiss you?"

"I think, if we're supposed to be madly in love—or at least wildly attracted to one another—you would have kissed me once or twice."

He managed to smile at that. "I definitely would have kissed you once or twice," he agreed. "And probably dozens of times more than that."

"So...will you do it?" she asked.

He wasn't sure it was a good idea. He also didn't see how he could answer her question in anything but the affirmative. Because she was right—if they were supposedly intimately involved and having a baby together, he would have kissed her at least once or twice before now.

"Alright," he agreed.

She smiled, apparently pleased by his response, and leaned over the center console, as if to facilitate contact.

"But not here," he told her.

She sat back again, frowning. "What's wrong with here?"

"Despite the fact that we're in the high school parking lot, we're not actually in high school anymore, and I'm not going to fumble around in a vehicle like a teenager."

"I wouldn't mind," she assured him. "I never experienced any back seat—or front seat—make-out sessions as a teenager."

"How did we go from a kiss to a make-out session?" he asked, not sure if she was being deliberately or innocently provocative.

Even in the dim light, he could see the blush that colored her cheeks.

Innocently provocative then, he realized—and wondered why he found that even more alluring.

"I'll take you back to your cousin's now and kiss you when we say goodbye at the door."

"Aren't you worried that Rafael will be watching through the window?"

"Worry about Rafael watching through the window will ensure a PG-13 rating," he told her.

"And not convince him—or anyone else—that we're passionately in love and desperate to get married," she pointed out.

"You're right." He unhooked his seat belt and exited the vehicle, then walked around to the passenger side and opened Winter's door. Following his lead, she unbuckled herself and slid out of her seat.

She looked at him, a combination of nerves and anticipation reflected in the depths of her dark eyes.

"Suddenly I'm as nervous as a teenager," she confided.

"It's just a kiss," he said, not entirely certain he believed it.

"Our first kiss—which will determine if this plan of yours is going to work."

"Now *I'm* nervous."

She smiled at that, though there was still a hint of wariness in her gaze.

"But actually, it's not our first kiss," Luca pointed out to her.

Winter dropped her gaze, a fresh hint of color filling her cheeks. "That was a long time ago... I wasn't sure if you remembered."

"I remembered."

"I think I'd be happier if you didn't."

"It was the night before you moved to Butte."

"We can skip the recap," she assured him.

"You came over to say goodbye to my sisters, hugged each of them and my parents, fighting back tears."

"I'd lived in Tenacity my whole life until then. I wasn't happy about the move," she pointed out.

"Your dad was supposed to pick you up, but he called to say that the moving truck had blocked him in and asked if my dad could give you a ride home. But I was heading into town, anyway... I don't remember why."

"You were meeting friends at the high school and then going to see a movie in Mustang Pass."

He nodded. "That sounds about right."

"Fast forward ten years, and here we are at the high school again."

"You fast-forwarded over the good parts," he admonished.

"There were no good parts."

"Before I met up with my friends, I took you home. I don't think you said two words to me throughout the drive. You just sat there, staring straight ahead out the window, your hands folded in your lap.

"The moving truck was still in your driveway, so I pulled up in front of the curb and said something lame like, 'good luck in Butte.'"

She chuckled softly. "Actually what you said was, 'have a hoot in Butte.'"

"More corny than lame," he acknowledged.

"No kidding. Those parting words went a long way toward helping me get over my crush on you."

"I didn't know you had a crush on me until you kissed me."

"An impulsive, desperate and not-at-all-romantic kiss."

"It was sweet."

She rolled her eyes. "You didn't even kiss me back."

"You surprised me," he said.

"I surprised myself," she admitted. "For weeks, I'd been dreading saying goodbye to you, heartbroken to think I'd never see you again."

"And here we are, more than a decade later," he mused. "Wildly in love and engaged to be married."

"Pretending to be wildly in love," she clarified.

"But actually engaged to be married, so we have to make our relationship convincing." He lifted a hand to her cheek, his fingertips sliding into her hair to the back of her head, tipping her face toward him. As his thumb stroked gently over the curve of her cheekbone, her eyes widened and her lips parted. "Which means making this kiss convincing."

"Which means you have to kiss me back this time."

"No." He shook his head. "*You* have to kiss *me* back this time."

He leaned closer.

She shivered.

"Are you cold?"

"No." She added a slight shake of her head to emphasize her response.

He brushed his thumb over her cheek again.

The tip of her tongue swept over the sensual curve of her top lip, moistening it.

He could see the awareness in her gaze, feel it in the hitch of her breath, even as his own blood began to heat in his veins.

She'd been married and was right now carrying a baby in her womb, so he knew she wasn't innocent. And yet, her responses to his touch, to his nearness, were instinctive rather than practiced. Guileless.

And incredibly arousing.

As he dipped his head, her eyes began to close.

"Look at me, Winter."

She did so, silently questioning.

"When I kiss you, I want you to know it's me who's kissing you," he told her. "Okay?"

"Okay," she agreed.

And she kept her eyes open as his mouth brushed over hers once, then settled.

Her breath whispered between her lips on a sigh.

A soft, sensual sound that arrowed straight to his loins.

He'd given her plenty of time to prepare for his kiss, and Winter felt certain that she was prepared—until the moment his mouth touched hers.

She'd been kissed by other men—most recently, by her now ex-husband. But no one, not even Matt, had ever kissed her the way Luca was kissing her. No one had ever made her body shift from slow burn to full blaze with just the brush of his mouth over hers.

And that was before he slid his tongue between her parted lips, deepening the kiss. She felt a quiver of something low in her belly—a quiver that slowly began to reverberate through her whole body, making her tremble and yearn.

She lifted her hands to his shoulders, holding on to him as the world tilted on its axis, making her knees weak and her head spin. One of his hands was still in her hair, but the other arm snaked around her middle, his palm splayed against her lower back, urging her closer to the hard length of his body.

And he was hard everywhere. Pressed up against him as she was, there was no way to miss the obvious evidence of his arousal. Which wasn't only a surprise to Winter but an incredible turn-on.

Luca's tongue danced with hers, a seductive rhythm that generated so much heat she wondered that her bones didn't melt. She'd never known a kiss could be so much—and somehow make her want so much more.

When he finally eased his mouth from hers, they were both a little breathless.

He held her gaze for a long moment as he drew air into his lungs, then he asked, "Does that answer your question?"

"I don't remember what the question was," she admitted.

His lips curved, but his eyes stayed locked on hers. "Whether we might be able to convince our families and friends that our relationship is real."

She nodded, her pulse racing. "I think we can."

"Let's find out," he suggested.

"We're getting married."

Luca made the announcement as he stood hand in hand with Winter in the living room of his parents' home.

"Married?" Will said, stunned.

"Married!" Nicole echoed, overjoyed.

They glanced, as one, from their son to his bride-to-be.

Luca gave Winter's hand a gentle squeeze of reassurance. She managed to nod and even smile a little.

Not exactly the picture of a woman head over heels in love, he acknowledged ruefully. Because she wasn't, though that was information he hoped to keep between the two of them.

"This is...unexpected," Will noted.

"Unexpectedly *wonderful*," Nicole insisted.

Apparently having four other children get married or engaged in the past twelve months had only intensified his mother's wedding fever.

Which, Luca realized now, could work in his favor.

"Did you have any thoughts on a wedding date?" Nicole directed this question to the bride-to-be. "June is nice, of course, but very popular."

"Actually, Winter's always dreamed of a winter wedding," Luca said, when his fiancée remained silent. "So we were thinking December."

"Even better," his mom said. "That will give us a whole year to make plans and—"

"Not next December," Luca interjected. "*This* December."

Nicole blinked, her enthusiasm momentarily overshadowed by surprise. "As in...this month?"

"Actually, we were hoping this week." He offered his most charming smile. "Maybe Friday?"

"*This* Friday?" She looked at Winter again, as if for confirmation. "That's...um...fast."

His bride-to-be, silent up to this point, finally found her voice and blurted out, "I'm pregnant."

And then she started to cry.

"Oh, honey. There's no need for tears." Nicole put her arm around her future daughter-in-law, eager to soothe her obvious distress even as she glared at her son. "But saying that, I remember those early days, when there were so many hormones wreaking havoc on my system, I'd cry at the drop of a hat."

"Glad to know it's not just me," Winter said weakly.

"It's definitely not just you," Nicole assured her. "Any pregnancy—and especially an unexpected pregnancy—can feel overwhelming."

"This one was definitely unexpected."

"But you want to marry Luca and have his child?" Nicole prompted gently, as if seeking reassurance that he hadn't bullied the expectant mother into accepting his proposal.

And the truth was, it had taken some creative thinking and fast talking to convince Winter to marry him, but Luca felt confident that they were doing the right thing for everyone concerned—and especially for the baby.

His bride-to-be looked at him now, emotion shimmering in her gaze. "I can't imagine anything more wonderful than having Luca's child."

And he felt an unexpected tug of regret that the baby she carried wasn't his.

After they shared the news of their impending nuptials with his parents, Luca took Winter back to her cousin's house.

"That actually went better than I anticipated," he told her, as they were en route.

She lifted a brow. "Even with my meltdown?"

He shrugged. "It's been an eventful day."

"It certainly has," she agreed. "And it's not over yet."

"You got a hot date or something?" he asked, obviously teasing.

"I have to call my parents. I don't want them to hear about our wedding plans from anyone else."

"Do you want me to make the call?"

She appreciated that he'd offered. And, truthfully, there was a part of her that desperately wanted to delegate the task to him. The part that knew her parents would be not only surprised by the news of her impending nuptials but disappointed in the reasons. Her parents had worked hard to give her opportunities, and she never wanted to disappoint them—but somehow she managed to do so, anyway.

But she needed to put on her big girl panties and deal with it. To prove to herself that she could stand up for herself, speak for herself. That she wasn't the helpless little woman incapable of making decisions that her ex-husband had almost managed to convince her she was.

"No." She shook her head. "It should be me."

"Do you want me to be there when you talk to them?"

She shook her head again. "I can do this."

"I have no doubt that you can do it," Luca said. "I'm only offering to be there to support you."

I have no doubt that you can do it.

His words surprised and warmed something inside her.

When was the last time anyone had expressed such unconditional belief in her?

She honestly couldn't remember. Certainly Matt had done his utmost to undermine her self-confidence, so that she second-guessed every decision she made. As she was already second-guessing this one now.

Did she really believe she could do this?

Convince her parents that she'd fallen in love with Luca and was having his baby?

Yes, she decided. She could and she would, because it was the only way to keep her baby safe.

So after Luca said good-night at the door and left her with a fleeting kiss that nevertheless stirred memories of their earlier lip-lock at the high school, Winter took out her phone and initiated a FaceTime call with her parents.

"How are things in Tenacity?" Josefina asked, after they'd exchanged greetings.

"Good," Winter said.

"Are you still working for Rafael?" Emilio queried.

"I don't actually work for Rafael," she reminded her dad. "I work at the same place where he works."

"A bar." Josefina sniffed disapprovingly.

"Rafael is a bartender," she acknowledged. "But Castillo's is a family restaurant, as you well know, because we used to eat there when we lived in Tenacity."

"You had a respectable job in Butte," her mom insisted. "And a husband."

"Now an ex-husband," Winter reminded her.

"You exchanged vows. You promised to love him until death."

"And he promised to honor and cherish me, and he broke those vows."

"Everyone makes mistakes."

Winter couldn't argue with that. Nor could she really blame her mom for not wanting to think the worst of her former son-in-law, because Matt had only ever been respectful and loving when her parents were around. It was only when they were alone that he took his frustrations out on his wife.

"I didn't call to talk about Matt," she said, determined to move the conversation forward. "I called because I have some news."

"What news is that?" her dad asked.

"I'm getting married again."

"You and Matt have reconciled?" Josefina's tone immediately shifted from disappointed to hopeful.

Winter resisted—barely—the urge to bang her head against the wall, aware that doing so wouldn't impact her mother's opinion at all but only give her a headache.

"She said she didn't call to talk about Matt," Emilio reminded his wife.

"Well, she's hardly had time to meet someone new, never mind fall in love," Josefina said.

"He's not someone new," Winter interjected, eagerly jumping into the opening she'd been given. "He's someone I've known a long time. And someone you know, too."

"Who is it?" Emilio asked cautiously.

"Luca Sanchez."

"Sanchez?" her dad echoed with a frown. "Would that be one of Will and Nicole's boys?"

Winter nodded. "Luca's the middle child and youngest son."

"The Sanchezes are good people," Emilio noted.

"That's hardly the point," Josefina argued. "It would be one thing if she said she was dating him, but getting married? It seems rather sudden—too sudden—to me."

"I can understand why you would think so," Winter said. "But you might remember that I had a crush on Luca when I was in high school, and when I came back to Tenacity, we reconnected."

"Not even divorced yet," her mother surmised, her tone filled with disapproval.

"My marriage was over long before the papers were signed, and when I saw Luca again, I realized that my heart was ready to move on."

"Maybe you think so now, but you shouldn't rush into anything," Josefina cautioned.

"Too late," Winter said.

Her mother's gaze narrowed. "What are you saying?"

"We're getting married on Friday and we're going to have a baby in June." She forced a smile. "You're going to be *abuelos*."

"A *bebé*," Emilio echoed, a slow smile spreading across his face. "*Que bendición.*"

"A baby with a man who isn't her husband," Josefina said disapprovingly.

"But he's going to be my husband," Winter pointed out.

"Vergonzosa. Pecaminosa."

"Josefina," Emilio said, gently admonishing. "There's no undoing what has been done. What matters now is that our daughter is having a baby with a man she loves. And it's neither embarrassing nor sinful that he is stepping up to do the right thing."

Winter didn't correct him—or maybe he hadn't said anything that needed correcting. Because the truth was, Luca had stepped up, even if it wasn't his baby. And if she wasn't in love with him, she was at least forever grateful to him.

"Only after doing a wrong thing," Josefina said.

Winter decided to ignore that, too.

"I'd really like it if you could be here for the wedding," she said instead.

"You expect us to come to Tenacity for a wedding that's happening in four days?" her mother said incredulously. "Your dad has an important job—he can't just take off on a moment's notice."

Winter ignored the stab of hurt that her mother's dismissive response evoked. "I don't expect anything," she said. "But I'm hopeful."

"We will see what we can do," Emilio promised.

"Gracias."

It had been an eventful day, Luca acknowledged, and all of it had started with a simple message from Winter.

He could have ignored her text.

Alternatively, he could have responded to her request in the negative.

And if he'd done either of those things, he wouldn't be staring at the ceiling now and wondering how in hell he was four days out from his wedding.

Instead, he could be wondering where Winter had gone, because she might already have left town, as she'd apparently made up her mind to do before he convinced her to give him time to come up with an alternative plan. Getting married was that plan, and as it had been entirely his idea, he could hardly blame anyone else for the current situation.

What had he been thinking?

What had compelled him to offer to marry a woman pregnant with another man's baby?

She hadn't expressed any concern about having a baby outside of wedlock—only that the timing of the birth would signal to her ex-husband that he was the father, and Luca could tell that she was sincerely afraid Matt would try to take her child.

Luca's single brief meeting with her ex-husband had been enough for him to see that Winter was unhappy in her marriage. It hadn't been easy for him to keep his mouth shut, but he'd forced himself to do so because her life was her own and not any of his business.

But she wasn't married to Matt Hathaway any longer. She was Luca's fiancée now—and soon to be his wife—and that meant she was his business. Not just Winter but also the baby she carried.

He'd come up with the marriage plan so that he could take care of and protect them both. But that was before he kissed her.

Before she'd asked him to kiss her.

It had been a simple request and not an unreasonable one. Unfortunately, kissing her had stirred wants and desires that were neither simple nor reasonable.

He'd offered to marry her so that she'd feel comfortable staying in Tenacity, where she could raise her child with the support of family and friends, and he knew that was why she'd accepted his proposal. The last thing she needed was a man who prioritized his own desires above her needs.

So if Luca was now feeling an inconvenient attraction to the woman who was going to be his wife, that was his problem to deal with. Unfortunately, he suspected that doing so would require a lot of very cold showers.

Chapter Four

"Are you sure your parents are okay with this?" Winter asked, as Luca loaded her belongings into the back of her SUV.

She was asking about the plan to move her in with the Sanchezes for the few days leading up to the wedding, so that she'd be onsite to help with the planning and preparations.

"It was my mom's idea," he told her. "Though she made it clear that you would sleep in Nina and Marisa's old room and I would sleep in mine and that there would be absolutely no sharing of a bed under her roof before we're married."

"And after we're married?"

"I've talked to my boss about renting another one of the cabins he keeps for married hands. He said he'll make sure he's got one ready before Friday."

"How do your mom and dad feel about that?"

"Are my parents okay with their thirty-one-year-old son moving out of their home and into a place of his own with his bride—is that what you're asking?"

She managed to smile at that. "I'll take that as a *yes*."

"The bigger question is—are Rafael and Sera okay with you moving out?"

"I think Sera's disappointed. She hoped having me in their basement would finally get Rafael to do some renovating. He's, of course, relieved to have that pressure taken off, and while he expressed some concern that our relationship is moving so quickly, he acknowledged that you're a much better choice than my ex-husband."

"Is that everything?" Luca asked, because he didn't think she wanted to hear his thoughts about her ex-husband.

"All my worldly possessions in two suitcases and three boxes," she confirmed.

"This is all that you took when you left Butte?"

"I didn't even take this much," she said. "Most of my clothes are from the secondhand shop here in town, because I didn't want anything that Matt had bought for me, seen me wear or even ventured to comment on."

"Gotta appreciate a woman who can travel light," he mused, again resisting the urge to express his real thoughts.

"For now, anyway," she agreed. "I've seen what Sera has to pack when she takes the baby out, and I wouldn't be surprised to learn that she was a sherpa in a previous life."

He chuckled at that, then, aware that Rafael or Sera might be watching through the window, touched a quick kiss to her lips. "I'll see you at the end of the road."

They got into their respective vehicles and set out.

When Luca ushered her into his parents' house twenty minutes later, Winter found her future mother-in-law at the dining room table with her two daughters.

Nina and Marisa sprang up from their chairs.

"I'm so happy that we're going to be sisters," Marisa said, hugging Winter close.

"I always thought you were too smart to give any of my brothers the time of day," Nina remarked, when it was her turn to embrace the bride-to-be. "But I'm excited to welcome you to the family, anyway."

"Thank you," Winter said, touched by their kind words and unquestioning acceptance of her presence in Luca's life.

"I'm Emery." This announcement came from a little girl

kneeling on a chair beside Nicole. "When you marry my Unca Luca, you'll be my Aunt Winter."

"Emery's mom is Ruby," Luca explained to her. "Julian's wife."

"Right." She nodded. "And you have a little brother, don't you?"

Emery bobbed her head. "Baby Jay. But he's more than a year old now, so Mommy says we should just call him Jay."

"Emery had a day off school today," Nicole told Winter. "So I invited her to hang out here."

"Aren't you a lucky girl?" Winter said.

She responded with another nod, ponytail bouncing. "I have three grammas." She held up three fingers. "Mimi, Gramma and Weyla."

Weyla—or *wela*—Winter guessed, was the little girl's version of *abuela*, a not uncommon form of the word.

"I hope you don't mind that I called in reinforcements," Nicole said. "But we've got a lot to do to get ready for the wedding and only a few days in which to do it, so I thought it would be helpful to delegate some of the tasks."

"We want to keep it simple," Luca reminded her. "A quiet ceremony with family and close friends."

"Your wedding day—simple or not—is one you'll remember for the rest of your life together," Nicole admonished her son. "And I'm not going to let you celebrate with music from your smartphone and pizza from Pete's."

"I like pizza," Emery said.

"Everyone likes pizza," Marisa assured the little girl.

"Unless, of course, that's what your bride wants," Nicole quickly amended.

"It's all about the bride," Nina said, winking at Winter. "So you tell us what you want, and we'll do everything in our power to make it happen."

"In three days?" Winter asked dubiously.

"If anyone can put a wedding together in three days, it's *Má*," Marisa assured her.

"I really don't mind keeping it simple," she said, looking helplessly at her future husband.

"Simple and beautiful," Nicole said with a nod.

"Let's start with the music for the ceremony," Marisa suggested. "Most brides opt for Pachelbel's 'Canon in D,' but I'm happy to play whatever you want."

"You're going to perform at the wedding?"

"Of course," Marisa said. "Unless you had somebody else in mind."

"No," Winter hastened to assure her. "And though I would never have asked, because it's a huge ask, it would mean so much to me—" she glanced at Luca "—to *us*, for you to play such an important part of our day."

"Yeah, I guess that's okay," he said, pretending he wasn't as pleased as his bride-to-be.

"Next on the list—flowers for your bouquet," Nicole said. "Did you have any thoughts?"

"Oh. Um." Her mind was blank.

"A hand-tied bouquet is simple but lovely," Nina chimed in.

"A hand-tied bouquet of red roses," Marisa suggested.

Roses?

Winter's stomach pitched at the thought.

"The color fits the season," Luca's youngest sister continued. "And red would contrast nicely with—"

"No," Winter interjected, managing to find her voice. "I don't want roses."

Nina frowned. "Why not?"

She sent an apologetic glance toward her future husband. "I had roses...the last time."

And it was the truth, if not the whole truth.

"No roses," her future mother-in-law immediately agreed.

Winter exhaled a quiet sigh of relief.

"What about carnations with seasonal greenery? And maybe some pinecones and berries?" Nina suggested as an alternative.

"That sounds perfect," she agreed.

"Flowers—check," Nicole said, ticking a box on her list.

"But what about the flower girl?" Emery asked.

"I didn't give any thought to a flower girl," Winter admitted.

"I was a flower girl when Mommy and Julian got married, so I know what to do," Luca's niece told her. "Plus, I already have a dress."

"Well then, it looks like we can check flower girl off the list, too," the bride-to-be said.

"Since I'm obviously not needed here…" Luca was already inching toward the door in an effort to make his escape.

Nicole consulted the paper in front of her. "Next on the list is cake."

"Chocolate," he said, pivoting back again. "With raspberry filling."

"Are you the bride?" Nina asked him.

"No, but shouldn't the groom get a vote?"

"What do you think, Winter?" Marisa asked.

"I'd prefer cherry filling," she said.

"I can live with cherry," he decided.

"Chocolate cake with cherry filling," Nicole said, recording the details on her checklist. "And now you're dismissed, Luca."

He frowned. "Why are you trying to get rid of me?"

"A minute ago, you were sidling toward the door," his mother noted. "I'm simply giving you permission to leave so you don't feel like you have to sneak out."

"When should I come back?" he asked.

"Dawson's picking up pizza at six."

"Everyone likes pizza," Emery said, echoing Marisa's words from earlier.

"I'll be back at six," he said, and disappeared, leaving his bride-to-be with his mother and sisters and niece.

"Is he gone?" Nicole asked, when the door closed at his back.

Nina went into the living room to peer out the front window. "He's pulling out of the driveway now."

"You *were* trying to get rid of him," Winter realized.

"Because I want to show you something," her future mother-in-law confided. "But if you don't like it, you can say so. I promise I won't be offended. And maybe it won't work anyway, but—"

"Mom," Marisa interrupted. "Just show it to her."

"Okay," Nicole said, and ducked out of the room.

Less than a minute later, she was back, carrying a long white dress on a padded hanger. It was a traditional satin ballgown with simple tank sleeves, a square neckline and sweep train.

"This was the dress I wore when Will and I exchanged our vows," Nicole said. "I thought you might want to wear it when you and Luca do the same, but it's okay if you don't."

Winter was touched and humbled by the generous offer.

"It's beautiful," she said. "And...white."

"Any bride can wear white," Nicole assured her.

"Even a recently divorced and now pregnant bride?" Winter asked dubiously.

"*Every* bride deserves to look and feel beautiful on her wedding day," her future mother-in-law insisted. "If you don't like the dress, that's fine, we'll find something else. But don't you dare think you're not entitled to wear it."

"It's beautiful," Winter said again. "But I also think you were a much slimmer bride than me."

"I wasn't blessed with your curves," Nicole admitted. "But if you like it, you can try it on and we'll see what kind of alterations might be needed."

So Winter tried it on, and though the bodice was a little snug—after zipping her up, Marisa had to undo the zipper immediately again to let the bride-to-be breathe—and the skirt a little long, Nicole assured her that the alterations could be made quickly and easily enough.

"When are your parents coming to town?" Nicole asked, as she gathered the skirt of the dress at the waist, lifting it to achieve the desired length.

"I'm not sure they're going to be able to make it," Winter confided.

Nicole's brow furrowed as she pinned the fabric.

"It's short notice," Winter explained. "And any requests my dad makes for time off have to go through the appropriate channels."

"Surely a request to attend his daughter's wedding would take priority," Nicole said.

"I hope so," the bride-to-be agreed. "But if it turns out that they can't make it, I could probably convince Rafael to give me away. But maybe it's silly to want someone to stand in for my dad. It's not likely I'll get lost if I don't have someone to walk me down the aisle."

Her future mother-in-law smiled a little, acknowledging her effort to make light of the situation, but her eyes remained troubled.

"If your dad can't make it and Rafael's unavailable, we'll find someone else to fill that role," Nicole assured her. "I have no doubt Will or Tío Stanley or even Julian or Diego would be happy to do the honors."

Winter had to swallow around the tightness in her throat before she could respond. "You've been so wonderful about everything," she said. "Even though I'm sure this isn't quite what you envisioned for Luca's wedding."

"To be honest, I hadn't let myself envision Luca's wedding at all, because I had no idea when—or even if—he might finally meet someone who inspired him to settle down." The groom's mom straightened up then and took the bride's hands. "I'm so pleased that someone is you."

"It doesn't bother you that I'm divorced?" she asked cautiously.

"Everyone makes mistakes in life. And if you weren't happy with your ex-husband, it would have been a bigger mistake to stay married."

"I wish my mother could see it that way."

"She'll come around," Nicole said.

"How do you know?"

"Because she loves you."

Winter knew that was true. And yet, she sometimes felt as if her mother expected too much of her—as if, because she was an only child, she was solely responsible for fulfilling all of her mother's hopes and dreams. And also the sole cause of all her disappointments.

"Could we maybe go for a walk?" Winter asked Luca Wednesday night, after dinner was finished, the kitchen had been tidied and his parents had gone to the living room to watch the evening news.

"A walk?" Luca echoed. "It's twenty degrees outside."

"A drive then?" she suggested as an alternative.

Though he still seemed puzzled by her request, he nodded. "Okay."

"We're going for a drive," he announced to his parents, as they made their way to the door to don boots and coats.

His dad lifted his hand in acknowledgment, his gaze not straying from the TV screen.

"Be safe," his mom said.

"Always," he promised.

He helped Winter with her coat, then took her arm to guide her to his truck.

"The ground's a little slick," he explained.

As if he needed an excuse to touch the woman he was scheduled to marry in less than forty-eight hours.

But maybe he did, because he hadn't made any efforts to do so since they'd shared the news of their engagement with their families, except for the express purpose of promoting their fake relationship.

"Anywhere in particular you want to go?" he asked, when he was settled behind the wheel.

"No," she said.

He backed out of the driveway and turned toward town. "Was there something you wanted to talk about?"

"Not specifically," she said, feeling suddenly and inexplicably nervous. "But I was hoping we could talk."

"And we couldn't do that back at the house?"

"I just thought it would be good to have some time alone—which has been in short supply since we got engaged."

"In the past two days, you mean? As we've been scrambling to get ready for our wedding?"

"I know we've both been busy," she acknowledged. "I just wanted to make sure there wasn't another reason that you might be avoiding me."

"I haven't been avoiding you," he promised.

"Okay," she said, choosing to believe him.

Because if she couldn't trust the man who was going to be her husband, why had she agreed to marry him?

"What else is on your mind?" he prompted gently.

"I guess I've been wondering if you're sure this is what you want to do—or if maybe you're having second thoughts."

"I made a promise to you when I put that ring on your finger," Luca said. "And I have no intention of breaking that promise."

"Which isn't the same thing as saying you want to marry me," she noted.

"It's true that marriage wasn't anywhere on my radar even three days ago," he admitted. "But now I'm committed to seeing this through—to being a faithful husband to you and a good dad to your baby."

"*Our* baby," she said. "If we want other people to believe you're the father, we need to show that we believe it."

His only response was a nod.

"I'm sorry if I dragged you out. I know you have to work early in the morning."

"It's seven thirty," he pointed out to her.

She felt her cheeks grow warm. "I thought it was a lot later."

"Might be because it gets dark so early this time of year. Or it might be that you're tiring more easily these days because your body's working hard to grow your—*our*—baby," he hastily amended.

"Someone's been reading up on pregnancy," she mused.

He shrugged. "Seemed like something an expectant father should do."

Which was only one more reason that she wished the baby she was carrying really was his.

"And on top of all that, you're planning a wedding, too," he noted.

"Your mom and sisters have been a huge help with that," she confided. "Honestly, I'm not sure there would be a wedding without them."

"As long as it's the wedding *you* want and they haven't imposed their own ideas and opinions," Luca said.

"It's the wedding I want, because I'm marrying you." And then, because she worried that simple but sincere statement might have given too much away, hinting at feelings she wasn't entirely ready to acknowledge even to herself, she added, "Because I know I'm safe with you. Me and our baby."

"You are safe with me." He glanced pointedly at the hand that covered the barely noticeable curve of her belly and nodded solemnly. "Both of you."

That was why she'd agreed to marry him—to give her baby

a father who would not only love but protect him or her. And she had no doubt that Luca would do that—and no right to ask for anything more. No matter how much her heart might yearn.

"Thank you," she said softly.

Now he shook his head. "You shouldn't have to be grateful to someone promising to treat you with the care and respect you deserve."

"And yet," she said softly.

"I haven't asked you for any details about your marriage," Luca pointed out. "Because what happened between you and your ex-husband isn't any of my business. Unless you want to talk about it, in which case, I'm here for you."

"I'm not unwilling to talk about it," Winter assured him. "Though I hate admitting that I was foolish enough to ever believe myself in love with him."

He put on his indicator and turned into the grocery store parking lot, pulling into a vacant slot and shutting off the ignition. He unbuckled his belt and shifted in his seat, giving his full attention to her.

"How did you meet?" he asked now.

"I was working as an office manager at DeSantis Construction in Butte and Matt was a sales rep for the company. And though I was initially reluctant to go out with someone I worked with, even indirectly, he was so attentive and charming that he eventually wore me down.

"We'd been dating only a few months when I found out that my dad was sick. Colon cancer. Thankfully, they caught it early and, because of an aggressive course of treatment, he's fine now.

"But in the beginning, not having a clue what his path forward was going to look like, I was a mess. And Matt was there for me. He took care of the little things so that I could focus on helping my parents.

"When he asked me to marry him, I was surprised. We hadn't been together that long, but he'd already quickly become an important part of my life, and I didn't hesitate to say *yes*. And when he suggested a quick wedding in Vegas, to ensure my dad could be there to walk me down the aisle, I said *yes* again.

"He knew all the right buttons to push to get me to relinquish control of my life to him without even realizing it."

"But you took that control back," Luca pointed out. "So instead of berating yourself for what came before, you should focus on and feel proud of that."

"I'm working on it," she told him.

"There is one other thing I'm curious about," he admitted.

"What's that?"

"The way you reacted when Marisa suggested roses for your bouquet... I got the impression there was more to it than carrying roses when you married Matt."

She nodded. "Once upon a time, roses were my favorite flower. Matt knew that, and at least once a month, he'd bring me roses. Alice, a friend who lived in the apartment across the hall, frequently remarked on his thoughtfulness in bringing me flowers. And not ready-made bouquets from the supermarket but carefully selected roses wrapped in fancy paper from the specialty flower shop.

"Because Alice believed the roses were Matt's way of saying, 'see how much I love you,' but I knew he was really saying, 'see how much I regret that you make me hurt you.'"

"How often did he hurt you?" Luca asked tightly.

"More than I want to admit," she confided. "He'd grab my arm, deliberately digging his fingers in. Or he'd squeeze my hand so hard that I'd wince. Sometimes he'd shake me or pull my hair. But he only ever hit me once."

"That's when you left," he realized.

She nodded.

"Can I ask..."

"Anything," she assured him.

"Why did you stay with him so long?"

She was quiet for a moment before responding. "Because I'd promised to love him, for better or for worse," she finally confided. "And if some days were worse than others, I figured that was just part of the deal.

"But when my parents moved to Dallas for my dad's promotion at the telecom company, the bad days started to outnumber the good. And I realized that having my parents in the same town had been a check on Matt's behavior, and when they were gone, so was that check."

"Did it surprise you that he didn't bother to respond to your divorce application?" Luca asked her now.

"It did," she admitted. "All I can think is that he didn't believe I'd go through with it. That, in the end, my fear of him would prove stronger than my desire to be free and I'd go back.

"I also suspect that when he got his copy of the divorce decree from the court, he was stunned to be proven wrong. But also unwilling, at that point, to admit he'd been wrong. Choosing, instead, to decide that he was better off without me."

"Unless and until he finds out that you're pregnant," Luca mused.

She nodded.

"Hopefully, once we're married, you'll be able to stop stressing about that and focus on your baby."

"Our baby," she reminded him. "Speaking of which, and since we're already here, would you mind if we popped into the store?"

"What do you need?"

"I don't *need* anything," she admitted. "But I've been craving ice cream all day."

"It's twenty degrees outside," he said again.

"I don't plan on eating it outside."

He pulled his keys out of the ignition. "Alright then. Let's go get your ice cream."

***

"When you said ice cream, I didn't realize you meant three different kinds," Luca commented, when they were on their way back to his parents' house.

"My favorite is black cherry with chunks of dark chocolate," she confided. "But the store didn't have that, so I went for the raspberry ripple. The chocolate fudge brownie is for the baby."

"You only discovered that you're pregnant three days ago and you're already catering to the baby's whims?"

"If you've been reading about pregnancy, you should know that cravings are real—and often the body's way to compensate for deficiencies in the mother's diet."

"You expect me to believe that you're deficient in...ice cream?"

"Dairy," she clarified.

"Which you could fix by drinking a glass of milk," he pointed out, as he parked.

"I'd rather have ice cream."

"And the mint chocolate chip?" he prompted, when he came around to the passenger side to give Winter a hand.

"Your mom's favorite. Or at least, it used to be."

"You remember that from more than ten years ago?"

She shrugged. "Marisa and I took driver's ed together, and we sometimes stopped for ice cream when your mom picked us up after class."

They removed their coats and boots by the door, then made their way to the kitchen.

"Anyone want ice cream?" Luca asked, as they passed the living room.

His dad's head swiveled; his interest obviously piqued. "What kind?"

"What kind do you like?" Winter asked him.

"Chocolate."

"We've got chocolate fudge brownie."

"Even better," Will said, rising from his recliner to join them in the kitchen.

"Mom?" Luca prompted.

She shook her head, not glancing up from the sock she was darning. "No, thanks."

"There's mint chocolate chip."

"And there goes my willpower," Nicole lamented.

And so Luca found himself seated at the kitchen table with his fiancée and his parents again, enjoying dessert and chatting about all manner of subjects that—surprisingly—had nothing to do with the upcoming wedding.

Winter talked to his dad about the plot twists in a recent *New York Times* bestseller that they'd both enjoyed and then transitioned to making plans to help his mom with her holiday baking.

His parents had always been kind to strangers and welcoming to friends, but there was a real warmth in their conversations with Winter that told Luca they both genuinely liked the woman who was going to be his wife. Which would obviously make for more comfortable family get-togethers and holiday gatherings, he noted with no small amount of relief.

And if it occurred to him that his bride-to-be fit into his world, as if the elusive "something" that had been missing from his life for the past decade was actually "someone" and that "someone" was Winter, well, that was a worry for another day.

Chapter Five

Winter was relieved when she got a text message from her dad, confirming that Emilio and Josefina would be in Tenacity for the wedding. She wanted to pick them up from the airport, but they opted to rent a car so they'd have transportation readily available when they were in town. Instead, they made plans to meet for lunch.

Since they would be dining at Castillo's, Winter decided she might as well put in a few hours in the office while she waited for them to arrive. She'd just finished calculating a stack of invoices when Roberto Castillo, Pablo and Yolanda's eldest son, knocked on the door.

"Your dad's here."

"Thanks, Roberto." Winter felt the smile spreading across her face as she saved her changes to the spreadsheet and closed the program.

Her father was standing by the bar, talking to Rafael, when she reached the main level. He immediately enveloped her in his arms.

She felt her eyes grow misty as she hugged him back. He'd always made her feel safe and accepted and loved, and she hadn't realized how much it meant to her to have him here for her wedding until right now.

"Where's *Má*?" she asked, when Dominic—a Castillo nephew who worked as a server—directed them to an empty booth.

"She asked me to drop her off at the church."

"Luca's brothers and sisters finished the decorating earlier today."

Emilio grimaced. "She didn't want to help with the decorating," he confided. "She wanted to pray."

"For my soul?" Winter guessed.

"Your mother has very strong feelings about the sacraments," he reminded her gently.

"And she still hasn't forgiven me for divorcing Matt."

"She struggles to understand how you could go from being head over heels in love with your husband to running away from him."

"I tried to explain it to her. She didn't want to listen."

Her father frowned at that. "What did you try to explain?"

She shook her head. "It doesn't matter now."

"It matters to me," he told her. "Why didn't you tell me you were unhappy in your marriage?"

"Because I'd made my choice when I exchanged vows with Matt," she said. "And I was prepared to live with that choice. But then... I just couldn't anymore."

"He hurt you," Emilio said. It wasn't a question. "I asked you about the bruises on your wrists and you said they were nothing."

"Because they were nothing—at least not in comparison to the bruises he left on my spirit."

Emilio looked devastated by this revelation. "You should have told me, *mija*."

"I was ashamed."

"He is the one who should be ashamed," her dad said fiercely.

"But I chose him," she acknowledged. "And when you urged me to get to know him better, to have a longer engagement, I refused to listen."

"You wanted to be sure that I would be there to walk you down the aisle," Emilio recalled.

She nodded. "You'd just started treatment and I was terrified of losing you."

"And yet here I am, ready to walk you down the aisle again."

"I wish this was the first time," she admitted.

"I wish this to be the last time," he said, softening the words with a smile.

"I didn't really know who Matt was when we exchanged vows," she confided. "But I know Luca—I know his character and his heart—and I want to be his wife, to share a home and a life with him and raise a family together."

"Then that's what I want for you, too." He reached across the table to touch her hand. "Be happy, *mi hija*."

"I will be. *I am*."

"Then I am happy to be here to celebrate with you." He pulled his hand back and patted his belly. "But I'll be even happier when our meals arrive—whatever it was they served on the plane was inedible."

"Prepare yourself for bliss, *Papá*," Winter advised, as Dominic approached with platters of food.

While Winter was having lunch with her dad, Luca was preparing to move out of his parents' home and into the cabin he'd rented for himself and his bride, also on Cedar Ridge Ranch.

He hadn't planned on living with his mom and dad forever, but he'd never had a compelling reason to move out before now. Sure, quarters had been a little crowded when his four siblings had all still been under the same roof, but it wasn't anything they weren't accustomed to. And when first Julian and then Diego moved out, Luca had felt like the king of his own castle in the bedroom he used to share with his two brothers.

It was strange to realize that he'd slept in this room almost every night of his thirty-one years and, stranger yet, to think that tonight would be his last night here.

"I've got another load of laundry for you," his mother said, carrying a stack of T-shirts into his room.

"Thanks."

"You want them in the box or the suitcase?"

"The suitcase, please."

She set the pile of shirts inside the case, and he saw her shoulders shake—just once—as she stood there for a minute, staring at the clothes he'd packed.

"Hey." He took her by the arms and gently turned her around to face him. "What's wrong?"

"Nothing." She wiped at the tears that had spilled onto her cheeks. "I'm just being silly."

"About what?"

She managed a small smile. "The last of my little birds leaving the nest."

"This little bird is thirty-one years old," he pointed out dryly.

"I know. And I'm happy that you've found a partner who loves you the way you deserve to be loved, who will build a home and a life and a family with you," she assured him. "I just didn't think it would happen so quickly."

"You know I've always been impatient. That when I find something I want, I don't like to wait."

"I hope that's the real reason you're in a hurry to get married," she said. "Obviously Winter's pregnancy is another, but I hope the baby is secondary to your feelings for one another."

"You don't need to worry, *Má*."

"It's a mother's job to worry," she told him. "Even when her nest is empty."

"You know all your birds come back to visit at every opportunity. And me and Winter won't be far away."

"I know." She brushed an errant tear aside. "But Christmas is in three weeks, and I've suddenly realized it will be the first time since Julian was born—almost thirty-five years ago—that it will just be me and your dad on Christmas morning."

"You might enjoy being able to sleep in for a change," he said lightly.

"Maybe," she allowed, though she didn't sound convinced.

"And we'll all be here to crowd around the table for dinner, as always."

"Are you sure about that? Have you talked to Winter about what she wants to do for the holidays?"

"Not yet," he admitted. "Most of our conversations of late have revolved around the wedding."

"Can I give you a piece of advice?"

"Of course."

"Don't make plans for Christmas—or anything else—without consulting your bride."

He frowned. "I can't think of any reason why she wouldn't want to come here."

"I'm not saying she won't," Nicole said. "But it's possible she'd prefer to spend your first Christmas as husband and wife alone together."

"Oh."

"Did that possibility really not occur to you?" his mom asked, sounding amused.

He shrugged. "I'm not used to factoring anyone else's wishes into my plans."

"Well, you better get used to it."

"I'll try," he promised.

"And she'll appreciate the effort." Nicole hugged him tight. "Now I'm going to bed so I don't have dark circles under my eyes at your wedding tomorrow."

"You also don't want to shed any tears at the wedding tomorrow," he admonished gently. "Or my bride might think you're not happy to welcome her to the family."

"Nothing could be further from the truth," she said. "In fact, if I could have chosen a bride for you, I would have chosen Winter."

"Someone like Winter, you mean?"

"No, I mean Winter," she assured him. "Because even when she was in high school with your sisters, when you pretended she was just a friend, there was always a spark between you."

Luca didn't dare question how his mom could have seen something that wasn't there, especially since he needed his parents to buy into the fiction that he and his bride were head over heels for one another. And if letting his mom believe they were meant to be together added weight to their story, he wasn't going to argue.

"Looks like the party got started without us," Diego noted, walking into the Grizzly Bar beside his brother.

The local watering hole was a classic style saloon with wood floors and a juke box that offered nothing but country music. But it had pool tables, for those who liked to play a game while they sipped their whiskey, and Dale Clutterbuck, the owner and chief bartender, generally kept his patrons in line with nothing more than his enormous size and usual stony expression.

"Party?" Luca echoed warily. "You didn't say anything about a party—just that you wanted to have a drink the night before my wedding."

"Because it's your bachelor party. And maybe we'll have one drink, maybe half a dozen drinks." His brother grinned. "We'll play it by ear."

"I don't want to be out too late," Luca said, as they joined their eldest brother, Julian, Winter's cousin, Rafael, and eighty-eight-year-old Great-uncle Stanley, already at the bar.

"We'll have you home before you turn into a pumpkin," Diego promised.

"Cinderella didn't turn into a pumpkin—it was the coach that took her to the ball that turned into the pumpkin," Julian corrected him. Then he noted his brothers' amused expressions and shrugged. "I read to Emery every night before bed, and she's into fairy tales right now."

"Robbie's still fascinated by *Goodnight Moon*," Diego said, referring to his fiancée's daughter.

"Lucky for you, that one isn't beyond your reading level." Luca couldn't resist teasing.

"Ha-ha."

"Bartender, pour the groom a shot of whiskey—and keep them coming," Stanley said.

Luca recognized the man behind the bar as Cameron Neill, who'd been in some of his classes in high school.

"Hold the whiskey and give me a beer instead," Luca said.

Cameron nodded and tipped a glass under a spout. "So it's true? You're getting married tomorrow?"

"It's true," he confirmed.

"Somehow the gossip mill jammed up on that one," the bartender mused. "I hadn't even heard that you were dating anyone."

"Then our efforts to keep our relationship under the radar were successful," Luca said.

"Under the radar and completely off the grid," Rafael grumbled.

"Because Winter was worried you might not approve of her dating so soon after her divorce," Luca told him.

"Winter…Hernandez?" Cameron asked, his interest piqued.

Luca nodded.

"Didn't she just move back to Tenacity a few months ago?"

"The beginning of September," Rafael said, glaring at his cousin's groom-to-be.

"That's some fast work," the bartender noted.

"Who's buying the drinks?" Luca's dad asked, making his way to the bar with Emilio Hernandez by his side.

Diego lifted a hand.

"Which is why I'll have another whiskey," Stanley said to the bartender.

Cameron dutifully poured the old man another drink.

"Beer for me," Will said.

"And me," Emilio added.

Luca only half listened to the conversations going on around him, his thoughts focused on one thing: He was getting married tomorrow.

It should not have been an earth-shattering revelation for a thirty-one-year-old man who'd always assumed his life would eventually take him in that direction. Because even if he hadn't been eager to make a lifelong commitment, he hadn't been opposed to doing so, either.

In addition to witnessing the example of his parents' marriage, Luca had watched each of his siblings fall in love and embark on a new life with their chosen partners—all within a calendar year. Perhaps it was those recent unions that had shone a spotlight on his solitary status, though he knew that feeling lonely was hardly a reason to dive headfirst into marriage.

Possibly Nina was right about him having a white knight complex. He'd always been protective of his family and friends, and though they'd lost touch for a lot of years, he still counted Winter as a friend. He would have wanted to help her in any way that he could, even before he realized she was in fear of her ex-husband.

Maybe he wouldn't be reeling over his impending nuptials if there had been a little more than four days between his proposal and the scheduled vows, he acknowledged. But even if his impulsive proposal had been a mistake, he could hardly back out now, less than twenty-four hours before the wedding. He couldn't—*wouldn't*—abandon Winter when he knew she was counting on him.

So resolved, he turned his attention to his future wife's cousin.

"Are you coming to the wedding?" Luca asked.

"I'll be there," Rafael confirmed. "I promised to be the getaway driver when she changes her mind."

"Not funny," Stanley admonished, shaking his head. "My bride disappeared on our wedding day, and it tore my beating heart right out of my chest."

"We all know the story, *Tío*," Julian said.

"You were there." The old man nodded now. "You helped me find her and bring her home. My Winona. *Mi ángel.*"

"I'm looking forward to meeting her at the wedding tomorrow," Emilio said to Stanley.

"You won't be able to miss her," Diego assured him.

"She does make an impression," Stanley agreed proudly.

"I just don't understand why anyone would want to jump into marriage again so soon after a divorce," Rafael remarked, circling the conversation back around to his cousin's wedding.

"Love is insplicable," Stanley said. "In-ex-plicable."

Rafael's grunt was noncommittal.

"And my daughter isn't going to change her mind," Emilio said, directing his comment to Luca now. "She knows her heart—and she's entrusting it to you."

"I'll be careful with it, sir," Luca promised.

"Give us another round, bartender," Stanley demanded, slapping the groom-to-be on the back.

Luca signaled Cameron with a subtle shake of his head. "I'm good, thanks."

"You're far too close to being sober," Diego said. "And at your own bachelor party."

"While I appreciate your willingness to pull out your wallet for a change, I don't think my fiancée would appreciate me being hungover on our wedding day."

Stanley shook his head despairingly. "Whipped already and not even married yet."

"And what's *your* bride going to think when you stumble through the door?" Will asked his uncle.

"That I had a good time celebrating my great-nephew's impending nupt'ls." The old man frowned. "Nuptals," he attempted to clarify the word. "Nup-ti-als."

So much had happened in the past four days that Winter hardly had a chance to catch her breath, never mind think about what she was doing. But now, the night before her wedding to Luca, there were so many thoughts spinning in her mind.

Too many thoughts and questions and concerns.

When she'd exchanged vows with Matt, she'd honestly believed it would be 4EVER—a sentiment he'd chosen to have engraved in their matching wedding bands. Unfortunately, her vision of wedded bliss was tarnished within four months and their marriage over within four years.

She had no doubt that leaving Matt was the right thing to do. Still, she hated feeling as if she'd failed. And she *had* failed. Not only when she walked out on her marriage, but also—and even more significantly—when she'd been unable to see beyond the charismatic exterior of the man who'd determinedly started to court her on her first day of work at DeSantis Construction.

Telling her parents that she was divorcing her husband had almost been harder than signing the papers. Josefina and Emilio had been married almost thirty-five years and—lucky for them—happily, because they didn't believe in divorce. To her parents, "till death do us part" meant exactly that, and they—or at least her mom—remained convinced that Winter and Matt could have worked through their problems if only they'd made the effort.

And the truth was, there were times that Winter wondered if maybe she hadn't tried hard enough. Because of course it was her fault that her marriage had fallen apart. At least that was what Matt wanted her to believe, as he'd held her responsible for everything that went wrong, not only in their marriage but in their everyday life. Even things she had absolutely no control over, such as the service tech for the internet provider company not showing up on time.

Not only did he blame her for everything, but he constantly derided her efforts and berated the results.

Why don't you listen to what I tell you?
Why do I have to tell you everything?
Why can't you use your brain?
Why are you so stupid?

Hearing those questions often enough, Winter had started to wonder the same things herself. She'd felt helpless and worthless—and pathetically grateful that he put up with a wife who was obviously so undeserving of him.

Getting away from Matt had been a lucky escape—and now, only a few months later, she was getting married again.

Do I really know Luca Sanchez any better than I knew Matt Hathaway?

Though she hadn't spent a lot of time with Luca in recent years, she'd known him since they were kids. Of course, she'd known Nina and Marisa better than any of their brothers, but she'd spent enough time in their home and with their family that she'd gotten to know Luca and Diego and Julian, too. And developed a huge crush on Luca in the process. Certainly she knew Luca's family better than she'd ever known Matt's family, and she knew that their home was filled with warmth and affection and love.

Nicole didn't tense when Will called out to announce that he was home, she didn't freeze up when her husband came near, and her hands didn't tremble with fear if she was late putting dinner on the table. They talked a lot, teased one another occasionally, and even bickered sometimes. But always, their interactions were underscored by genuine affection and mutual respect.

Though Winter's own parents maintained more traditional roles in their marriage, she would also characterize their relationship as loving and supportive. And because she'd never witnessed anything different, she'd foolishly believed her marriage would be the same.

She hadn't seen the signs when she was dating Matt.

Or maybe she'd just been too stupid to recognize them.

No, not stupid, she decided, dismissing the label Matt liked to slap on her. Just naïve. Innocently and blissfully naïve.

She wasn't naïve anymore, and she was going into this marriage with her eyes wide open.

Luca hadn't offered her any flowery declarations of love or made any extravagant promises about the life they'd have together. He'd simply looked at the problem and offered a solution—his name on her baby's birth certificate.

And in less than twenty-four hours, the man she'd seriously crushed on in high school was going to be her husband.

Was it any wonder that she was uneasy and unable to sleep?

Which was the reason she was in the kitchen, warming a cup of milk in the microwave, when she heard voices outside the door.

Luca and his dad, she realized.

Nicole had told her that Julian and Diego were taking Luca out for a boys' night before the wedding, and maybe that knowledge had contributed to her sleeplessness, too. Maybe she'd worried that being out with his brothers—and apparently his dad and her dad, too—the night before their wedding would put too much focus on The Big Day and lead him to wonder if his offer to marry her hadn't been A Big Mistake.

Though she couldn't make out the words, she heard the murmurs of their conversation as they came into the house, then went their separate ways. Will to the room he shared with his wife on one side of the house and Luca to his childhood bedroom on the other. It was only Luca's path that took him past the kitchen, where she was now sipping her drink.

He didn't notice her right away, which gave her a minute, unobserved, to look at him and appreciate that the boy she'd once known was now definitely a man.

She'd always thought Luca handsome, and he'd only grown more so in the years that she'd been away from Tenacity. His broad shoulders were no doubt a side effect of the physical labor he performed every day, as were the taut muscles that filled out his lean frame. His face had matured, too, with faint lines at the corners of his eyes and mouth—evidence of his ability to find humor in almost any situation and his quickness to smile. His hair was a little longer now, flirting with his collar and falling carelessly over his forehead, and his jaw was frequently unshaven, adding to the slightly rough-around-the-edges look that she realized, with some surprise, she liked.

Or maybe what she liked was that he didn't pretend to be anyone other than who he was. The son of a ranch hand and a seamstress, now a ranch hand himself. An inherently good man with simple values and strong moral fiber. Steady, loyal, dependable and protective of those he loved.

Winter knew she didn't fit into that category. He didn't love her, but he was going to marry her, anyway, and she knew he'd protect her and her baby.

Their baby.

She was making a conscious effort to think of the tiny life in her womb as their child, because Luca would be the baby's father in every way that mattered. She was so grateful to him for everything he was doing for her—and uncomfortably aware that he was getting nothing in return.

Was that why she couldn't sleep the night before her wedding?

Was her conscience only now waking up and letting her

know that it would be unforgivably selfish to go through with the exchange of vows?

Or was she simply experiencing proverbial cold feet?

Or possibly—secretly—afraid, because she knew only too well how quickly dreams could turn into nightmares?

"Winter," Luca said, pausing in mid-step. "What are you doing up?"

She gestured with her mug.

He came closer to peer at the contents of her cup. "Warm milk?"

She nodded.

He made a face.

"You drink warm milk," she pointed out.

"Only if it's mixed with lots of cocoa powder and sugar."

"You put something else in your hot cocoa," she mused. "A secret ingredient."

"That's true," he confirmed.

"What is it?"

"If I told you, it wouldn't be a secret."

"A husband shouldn't keep secrets from his wife," she chided.

"So ask me again, after we're married," he suggested.

"And you'll tell me?"

"If it's a marriage rule that spouses should have no secrets, then I'll have to tell you," he said. "But after that, there'll be no reason you can't make your own hot cocoa."

"Maybe I don't need to know," she decided.

He smiled then. "You want me to upgrade that warm milk in your cup to hot cocoa now?"

She hesitated, then shook her head. "It's late. You probably want to get to sleep. And I should, too."

"Weren't you drinking warm milk because you were having trouble sleeping?"

"Apparently your deductive reasoning skills aren't negatively impacted by alcohol consumption," she said lightly.

"I had one beer."

"Oh."

"I've never been much of a drinker," he confided. "And I didn't want to be less than one hundred percent tomorrow."

"Tomorrow," she echoed softly.

"Our wedding day."

She nodded. "Right."

He waited patiently for her to follow-up with something else, but there were so many thoughts spinning around in her head she couldn't seem to latch on to any one.

I'm getting married again.

Tomorrow.

Luca will protect my baby.

Our *baby.*

He'll give up his own future for us.

I can't let him give up his future.

I have to leave Tenacity.

The thoughts, still spinning, were joined now by spots of light dancing behind her eyes.

Spinning and dancing and—

Chapter Six

"Breathe."

Winter blinked. "What?"

"You weren't breathing," Luca said, carefully removing the mug from her hands.

"Oh." No wonder she felt dizzy and light-headed. She pressed her hands to her warm cheeks and focused on drawing air into her lungs and pushing it out again.

"Better?" he asked, after she'd taken several breaths.

She nodded.

"Second thoughts?" he asked gently.

She looked at him, wondering if he could see in her eyes the fear and regret and apology that filled her heart.

She nodded again. Slowly. Reluctantly.

"So let's see if we can work our way through them," he suggested reasonably.

"And if we can't?"

"If we can't…then we call off the wedding."

"Just like that?"

He shrugged. "You recently ended one marriage. People would understand that you're not ready to jump into another one so quickly."

Maybe he was right. And the realization that she was, in fact, free to change her mind caused relief to rush through her.

She didn't have to put on Nicole's wedding dress and go to the church and exchange vows with Luca.

She didn't have to do any of it.

It was her decision to make.

But if she didn't go through with it, if she didn't marry Luca, she'd be right back in the same untenable position she'd found herself in three days earlier—although no longer locked in a bathroom, staring in panicked disbelief at the results of a pregnancy test.

Because Luca had offered a helping hand—not a controlling one.

"Being married to you wouldn't be anything like being married to Matt," she acknowledged. "Besides, your parents and siblings have all gone to so much trouble to make this wedding happen."

"It wasn't trouble," he denied. "They were happy to do it."

"They won't be happy if we don't go through with the wedding. Neither will mine, especially my mom, who wasn't exactly thrilled to have to rearrange their schedules to be here."

"We're not getting married to make our parents happy," he pointed out.

He was right.

The sole reason for this wedding was to give her baby a father—and to protect the tiny life inside her from the man who'd actually contributed DNA to its creation.

"It's your call, Winter," Luca promised.

"I'm not sure I can be trusted to make the right decision," she said, not entirely joking.

"It's not about right or wrong—it's about whether you want to get married tomorrow or not."

Do you even have a brain in that head of yours?

Answer me, dammit.

"Hey." Luca tipped her chin up, his brow furrowed.

His touch was gentle, his expression concerned, reminding her once again that her future husband was nothing like her ex.

"There's no pressure, Winter. You get to decide what you want to do."

She appreciated what he was saying, but he was wrong. There was nothing but pressure because her options were limited. She either married Luca and potentially ruined his life or she reverted to plan A—moving away from Tenacity and raising her baby alone.

"I want to marry you," she said. "For all the reasons previously discussed. But it's occurring to me now that you might have your own reasons for wanting to back out of our wedding."

"I have no intention of backing out," he assured her.

"Maybe you should reconsider," she suggested. "You're sacrificing so much for me."

"What is it that you think I'm sacrificing?" he asked curiously.

"The chance to fall in love and make a life with that person."

"I'm going to make a life with you and your baby."

"*Our* baby," she reminded him. "Which isn't even close to being the same thing."

"Did you love Matt?" he asked her now.

"Touché."

"Maybe love is the icing on the cake," Luca said. "But the cake is what really matters. It's the foundation of caring and trust and respect that supports everything else in a marriage."

"What does the cherry filling represent?" she asked lightly.

"The unexpected sweet surprises that come from sharing a life with someone else."

"Like a baby born five months after the wedding?"

"I was thinking more along the lines of a smile across the breakfast table in the morning, sharing a bowl of popcorn while watching a movie, someone to walk with under the stars or who will make you hot cocoa on a cold night. But yeah, I'd say a baby counts as a sweet surprise, too."

And those simple words melted the last of the barriers around her heart.

"Thank you," she said softly.

He pressed his lips to her forehead. "Think you can sleep now?"

She nodded.

And when she went back to her bed, she did sleep—and dreamed of him.

Luca wasn't really surprised to learn that his fiancée was having doubts. He'd had a few of his own, and he'd never been down this road before to be as familiar with the bumps and ruts as Winter obviously was.

"You keep looking at your watch," Diego commented, as the brothers waited in the vestibule of Goodness & Mercy Nondenominational Church, where Luca and Winter's wedding was to take place. "Is that because you're wishing time would go faster? Or slower?"

He responded by pulling his sleeve over his wrist, hiding his watch from view. "Has anyone seen Winter?"

"She's in the anteroom with Nina," Julian said.

"How do you know?"

"Well, that was the plan," his eldest brother reminded him.

"I didn't ask what the plan was—I asked if anyone had seen her."

"Worried that she might do a runaway bride?" Diego couldn't resist teasing.

The groom glared at his middle brother.

"Come on, *mano*. You can't honestly have any doubts about a woman who's clearly head over heels for you."

Luca didn't know what might have given his brother that impression, but he knew it couldn't be further from the truth.

"And even if she wasn't, she's pretty much stuck after letting you knock her up."

Diego was teasing, of course, and being obnoxious about it because that's what brothers did. And though Luca and Winter had agreed to keep the news of her pregnancy quiet for now, they'd obviously made an exception for family who might otherwise have expressed concern about the hasty nuptials.

Still, Luca couldn't help but wish he'd been able to tell his brothers the whole truth about his fiancée's baby. Both of them were in relationships with women who had children with other men, and he thought they might be good sounding boards going forward. But Winter had been adamant that nobody could know the truth about her baby's paternity, and he would never betray her confidence.

"Nina just confirmed that Winter is in the anteroom," Julian said, tucking his phone away again. "And the father-of-the-bride just showed up there, too."

"I guess that means it's showtime," Luca said, and prepared to play the most important role of his life.

On her way to the anteroom, where the bride traditionally waited for the ceremony to begin, Winter had caught a glimpse inside the nave and been amazed at the transformation effected. Nina and Barrett, Marisa and Dawson and Diego and Jenna, his fiancée, had been conscripted by Nicole to decorate the church, and they'd gone full-scale holiday theme with yards and yards of holly garland, hundreds of twinkly white lights and dozens of potted poinsettias. It was the winter wedding she'd always dreamed of—or it would have been if the bride and groom had been madly in love and marrying for all the right reasons.

But if she and Luca weren't doing this for the right reasons, they were at least doing it for compelling reasons.

When she saw him standing at the front of the church, her heart gave a little flutter inside her chest. And for just a moment, she let herself pretend that this really was a love match. That her groom cared about her as much as she'd always cared about him and they weren't only getting married to protect her unborn child from her ex-husband, but because they wanted to build a life and a family together.

Because wasn't that the fairy tale of every bride?

And apparently Winter wasn't any different, despite knowing only too well that fairy tales didn't exist outside the pages of storybooks.

Her glance shifted then to Will and Nicole in the first row, smiling and holding hands. On the other side of the aisle was her mom, watching her husband as he walked their daughter down the aisle.

At the front of the church, Julian and Diego stood beside Luca. But her attention was drawn back to her groom, so breathtakingly handsome in his formal attire that her heart fluttered again.

On Winter's side of the altar stood Sera and Nina and Emery, who'd marched confidently down the aisle ahead of the bride, scattering white hydrangea petals like the experienced flower girl she'd assured the bride she would be.

When Winter reached the front of the church, her dad kissed her on both cheeks before turning to offer a hand to her groom. After Emilio was seated beside Josefina, the minister began.

"Dearly beloved, we are gathered today, in the sight of God and the presence of family and friends, to celebrate the love of Luca Sanchez and Winter Hernandez as they come together in marriage…"

She must have responded appropriately when it was her turn to do so, because the next words she heard the minister say were, "You may kiss your bride."

She looked at Luca then.

He smiled, as if there was nothing he wanted more. As if this wasn't just the last ceremonial hurdle to get over to finish the ceremony.

She held her breath, waiting for the touch of his lips, grateful that they'd practiced this part.

Not specifically a wedding kiss but holding hands and exchanging casual touches so they would appear comfortable with one another and such simple displays of affection. She felt confident it had worked, because she no longer jolted when he reached for her hand or froze when he slid an arm across her shoulders. And if everything inside her melted at his closeness or her heart pounded wildly in her chest…at least those instinctive responses weren't evident to anyone but her.

He'd stepped up to help her out when she needed it. Going above and beyond anything she might have imagined, offering her not only a solution to her current dilemma but also reviving a long-dormant teenage dream in which he'd look at her like someone he might be interested in and not just one of his sisters' friends. Look at her and then take her in his arms and kiss her…

As he was kissing her now, she realized.

Softly and sweetly.

Lingering just long enough to make their wedding guests—and her heart—sigh.

When he lifted his lips from hers, there was a smattering of polite applause.

"Ladies and gentlemen, let me be the first to introduce to you Mr. and Mrs. Luca Sanchez…"

After the ceremony, they had some photos taken at the church with family and friends, then the bride and groom joined their guests for a celebration at the Tenacity Inn. The local Social Club, a popular choice for wedding receptions, hadn't been available and the booth-style seating at Castillo's had ruled out the restaurant as an alternate venue. Thankfully, Julian's wife, Ruby, who worked at the inn, had been able to bump a conference group to another meeting room, freeing the largest space for the wedding party.

Obviously Winter hadn't been paying enough attention when Luca's mom and sisters were talking about the schedule of events for the day, because she hadn't given a single thought to dancing until her new husband offered his hand.

"They're playing our song," he said, as the first notes of John Legend's "All of Me" spilled out of the sound system.

"Is this our song?" she asked.

"Since it will be the first song we ever dance to, I suppose that makes it ours."

"A good choice," she said. "I used to listen to this song over and over again in high school."

"That's probably why Marisa chose it for our first dance."

"Prior to the announcement of our engagement, I hadn't exchanged more than a handful of words with either of your sisters since moving back to Tenacity," she confided, feeling more than a little bit guilty about the fact. "And still, Marisa and Nina jumped right in, helping in any way that they could to make this day happen."

"You're a Sanchez now," Luca noted. "Which means you're stuck with them forever—even when they get on your last nerve."

She smiled at that, even as she found herself wondering if he really meant it. If he really thought their marriage would last forever.

Not that she was looking for an exit door only hours after the exchange of vows, but she'd been so focused on the wedding she hadn't given much thought to the potential longevity of their marriage.

Those thoughts slipped from her mind when he splayed his other hand on the small of her back and drew her closer to the heat of his body. Her heart started to pound harder and faster, echoing in her head so that she could barely hear the song that was playing. But maybe that didn't matter. Maybe it was enough to follow Luca's lead, to focus on the man rather than the music.

"I didn't have a chance to tell you earlier, but you look absolutely spectacular today."

Winter smiled, a little shyly. "It's your mom's dress."

And now he knew why it looked somewhat familiar, because he'd seen photos of his parents' wedding. But his mom hadn't filled out the dress like Winter did.

"It looks...different on you," he said inanely.

"Your mom's taller than me—and not as curvy, so she made some alterations," his bride acknowledged. "To be honest, I was a little worried it wouldn't fit today, because even in the few days that have passed since I first tried it on, I've noticed changes to my body. My belly is slightly rounded now and my breasts are fuller—and I can't believe I just said that to you."

"You can say anything to me—there aren't supposed to be any secrets between a husband and a wife, remember?"

"At the opposite end of the spectrum from keeping secrets is oversharing."

"Would it be oversharing if I said that your fuller breasts look absolutely stunning in that dress?"

"It definitely would," she agreed, but her admonishment was softened by the smile that curved her lips.

Though Winter was a little disappointed to have to leave her husband's arms after only one song, she was grateful, too, because being close to Luca had stirred up all kinds of unexpected—and unwelcome—questions, most of which involved potential activities for later in the evening.

After the bride and groom's first dance, Winter took a turn around the floor with her dad while Luca led his mom to Phil Collins's "You'll Be in My Heart." It was a beautiful song, and Winter teared up a little as she danced with her dad—or maybe it was just all the emotion of the day catching up with her.

"Those better be happy tears," Emilio said. "I don't want to have to kick your new husband's ass already."

She chuckled softly. "Definitely happy tears," she assured him. "This whole day has been more wonderful than I could have imagined."

"I'll admit I had some concerns when you called and told us about your plans to get married again—and so quickly," her dad confided. "You alleviated most of those concerns at lunch yesterday, but today, seeing you with Luca, I'm further reassured. It's obvious there is genuine attraction and affection between you, and I feel confident that you're going to have a long and happy life with your husband and child—and hopefully many more babies in the future."

"I didn't realize you were so eager to be an *abuelo*," Winter said, because she didn't want to focus on the rest of his comment, didn't want to feel proud that she'd managed to fool her parents into thinking that her marriage to Luca was the real deal.

Because she needed them to believe it.

She needed her family and Luca's family and all the residents of Tenacity to believe that they were head over heels in love before the news of her pregnancy spread, so no one would have cause to question the paternity of her baby.

But the truth weighed heavily in her heart, and she hated knowing that she'd dragged a good man into the middle of her mess.

Not that she'd had to drag Luca.

He'd jumped feetfirst.

And she would always be grateful to him for his willingness to do so.

"It's been a long day, hasn't it," Luca asked several hours later, when he caught his bride stifling a yawn.

She nodded. "Unfortunately, it doesn't look as if this party is even close to winding down."

"I don't think anyone will mind if we duck out. They'll just assume we're eager to be alone together."

She realized he was alluding to the consummation of their marriage, and despite the fact that he hadn't given any indication of wanting a proper wedding night, she felt her cheeks grow warm.

"Not so fast," Julian said, stepping forward with his wife to block the newlyweds' escape at the door.

"You can rib me about being a party pooper tomorrow," Luca told his brother. "Right now, I'm taking my tired wife home."

"I hope you're not too tired," Ruby said to Winter, with an exaggerated wink. "Because we've got a surprise for you."

"What's this?" Luca asked, when his sister-in-law handed him an envelope.

"Our wedding gift to you," Ruby announced, looking pleased with herself.

"You guys didn't have to get us a gift," Winter protested.

"Of course, we did," Julian said.

Luca lifted the flap of the envelope and pulled out...a keycard.

"That's your access to the honeymoon suite," Ruby told him.

"The inn has a honeymoon suite?"

"It's not officially a honeymoon suite," she acknowledged. "And not as fancy as what you'd find at an upscale hotel in a big city, but it's the nicest room on the top floor to which we've added some special touches for the occasion."

"You really shouldn't have gone to the trouble," Winter said.

"How many times does a bride get to experience her wedding night?" Ruby asked.

"Other than the first time, you mean?"

Luca's sister-in-law blushed. "I should have been able to avoid stepping in that one, because I was married before, too. Perhaps what I should have said is, how many times does a bride get to experience her first night married to a Sanchez? Because I have no doubt Luca will make it unforgettable."

Winter hoped the flush she felt didn't show on her cheeks. "It's a thoughtful and generous gift, but I don't even have a toothbrush—"

"There are complimentary toiletries in the bathroom."

"Or a change of clothes for the morning."

"Nina packed a bag for you, and Diego packed one for Luca. Both have been taken upstairs already."

"Looks as if you've thought of everything," Luca said.

Ruby beamed proudly.

"I can't think of any reason we shouldn't enjoy your generous gift." Winter even managed a small smile before she looked at her new husband and asked, with just a hint of desperation in her tone, "Can you?"

"No reason at all," he confirmed with false cheerfulness.

Chapter Seven

So the newlyweds thanked Julian and Ruby again and hugged them both, then dutifully headed to the elevator that would take them to the honeymoon suite.

"This is…unexpected," Winter noted, as the doors opened.

"That's one word for it," Luca agreed.

He stepped into the car with her, then punched the button for the top floor.

"You don't seem pleased by your brother and sister-in-law's gift."

"I don't like surprises."

"Good to know," she responded lightly.

He exited the elevator and made his way down the hall, pausing at the room whose number matched what Ruby had printed on the envelope. He waved the key card in front of the lock and, when the light blinked green, pushed open the door and gestured for Winter to precede him.

He didn't need to turn on the lights, because there were candles—dozens of candles around the room—already lit, their flickering flames adding warmth and ambience. There was a sitting area on one side of the room, with a couple of wing chairs flanking a small table and facing a flat-screen TV mounted over an electric fireplace. On the table was a bottle of nonalcoholic sparkling wine in an ice bucket, two crystal flutes and a board with an assortment of cheeses and crackers and fruit. But the centerpiece of the room was the huge four-poster bed covered in rose petals arranged in the shape of a heart.

"Somebody went to a lot of trouble," Winter mused.

"There's only one bed," Luca said, stating the obvious.

She nodded. "At least it's a big bed."

And at the foot of the bed were two duffel bags, one with a tag labeled "bride" and the other denoted for the "groom."

"I realize this situation is beyond awkward," she continued. "But maybe we should take this as a positive sign."

"Of what?" he asked dubiously.

"That we've managed to convince people our relationship is real."

"It is now," he confirmed.

"Or at least legal."

He gestured to the snacks in the sitting area. "Are you hungry? Thirsty?"

She shook her head.

"Want to watch a movie?"

"Anything to avoid getting into that bed with me, huh?" she teased lightly.

"You're tired," he said.

"Definitely ready to get out of this dress and into my pjs."

"Okay."

"But I'm going to need some help."

He swallowed. "Help?"

"With the zipper," she told him.

"Oh. Okay."

She turned around, so that her back was to Luca.

He found the tab of the zipper at the top of the dress and slid it downward, per her request.

He could smell Winter's hair—or maybe her skin—something tropical and warm that stirred his blood.

The zipper inched lower, revealing a glimpse of pale, smooth skin. Another few inches exposed the white lace band of her bra.

He swallowed. "Do you want it unzipped all the way?"

"Yes, please."

It was so quiet in the room, he could hear the rasp of the teeth parting as he slid the tab lower. With each inch, more creamy skin was revealed. Then the lacy edge of panties that obviously matched her bra.

He didn't think she'd worn the sexy lingerie to entice him. More likely, they were simply appropriate undergarments for a wedding dress.

But he was definitely enticed.

Aroused, even.

"Done," he announced in a strangled tone, forcing his hand to drop away from the zipper.

"Thanks."

"Anything else you need?" he asked, because apparently he was a glutton for punishment.

"Actually, yes," she said. "Could you help with my hair?"

"You got a zipper hidden somewhere in that fancy twist?"

"Unfortunately, no," she said wryly. "Just about a thousand pins."

"What do you need me to do?"

"Can you find them and take them out?"

"I'll give it a go," he promised, studying the intricate twists of glossy dark hair studded with decorative pearls.

It was only when he'd removed all the pearl-tipped pins that he realized there were a lot more pins hidden in her tresses to hold the style in place. Probably not a thousand, but a lot. And it was easier to feel them than see them, so he let his fingers slide through the silky strands to search for and remove them.

"Let me know if I'm hurting you," he said, as he worked a tangled pin free.

"You're not," she promised.

He found another pin; she sighed with pleasure when it was gone.

"Mmm," she hummed, as his fingertips massaged her scalp.

"Ohh," she sighed, as another pin was pulled free.

Three more pins were located and removed from the top of the knot, and her hair tumbled free.

"Mmm." She hummed her appreciation again as the long tresses spilled over her shoulders and down her back. She gave her head a slight shake. "That. Feels. So. Good."

He'd heard those words before, though usually in more intimate situations—and definitely not something he should be thinking about now. But it had been difficult to focus on the task at hand while she'd been making what could only be described as sex noises the whole time he'd been plucking pins out of her hair. And more difficult still when those noises had caused all the blood to drain from his head and settle in his boxers.

"Thanks," she said again, before grabbing the "bride" duffel and ducking into the bathroom.

Luca didn't turn until he heard the door close for fear she would notice the massive erection tenting his pants. Only then did he make his way around the room, blowing out the candles and snuffing out the romantic ambiance.

After that, he punched the power button on the remote to turn on the TV. He scrolled through the channels until he found an episode of a sitcom he'd likely already seen a dozen times and tried not to listen to the sound of water running in the bathroom. Just the faucet, thankfully. He didn't think he could handle thinking about Winter stepping naked under the spray of the shower.

But of course he was going to have to. This one night in the honeymoon suite was only the beginning. When they checked out of the inn in the morning, they would head to their own cabin, where they would live together as husband and wife.

Or at least a passable imitation of husband and wife.

When he'd promised to be with her "for better or for worse," he hadn't anticipated that the worse part would be wanting her and not being able to touch her.

***

The first thing Winter did when she escaped into the bathroom with her duffel bag was step out of Nicole's wedding dress and carefully hang it on the hook on the back of the door. Then she removed the layers of makeup from her face, applied moisturizer to her freshly washed skin, worked the tangles out of her hair and brushed her teeth.

Rummaging through the contents of the duffle, she found a bra, socks, underwear, jeans and a sweater—obviously her outfit for the next day—but no pajamas. There was, however, a small gift-wrapped box beneath the clothes.

She pulled it out and glanced at the handwritten tag.

From your sisters, with best wishes for your wedding night and always. xoxo

Touched, and just a little bit wary, she tore away the paper and opened the box to reveal an elegant—and very sexy—chemise and peignoir set.

She lifted the chemise out of the box and held it up in front of the mirror.

She certainly couldn't fault Luca's sisters' taste, and if she'd been looking for something seductive to wear on her wedding night, she might have chosen something just like this. It had tiny straps with strategically placed lace embellishments on a sheer V-neck bodice that descended to a flowy silk skirt. The cover at least was the same whisper-thin silk as the skirt, which meant that it wouldn't leave much to the imagination but at least it wasn't see-through.

As if the one bed situation wasn't awkward enough, now she was going to have to get into that bed—with her husband!—wearing a garment designed for seduction rather than sleep.

And he hadn't given her any reason to think he might want to consummate their marriage. In fact, aside from the one passionate kiss they'd shared the night he'd put his ring on her finger, he'd given no indication that he might be the least bit attracted to her.

Well, there was the flirtatious comment he'd made on the dance floor about her fuller breasts, but she knew he'd only been trying to make her feel better about her own oversharing. She also knew that he never would have made such a comment if they hadn't been in a public space, where the presence of friends and family ensured a little playful banter wouldn't lead to anything more.

But they were alone now.

Alone in a hotel room with one bed.

The silky fabric of the chemise caressed her skin as it fell into place, making her yearn for a man's caress.

Luca's touch.

If wishes were horses, she mused, as she belted the peignoir.

Still, her heart was racing as she reached for the knob of the door…

When he heard the bathroom door open again, Luca glanced over his shoulder, determined to play it cool. He did a double take when he saw his bride wearing a silky wrap with a tie around the waist that emphasized her delectable curves. He tried his best not to ogle, but—*santo infierno*—he could not tear his eyes away.

She'd been wearing pajamas when he found her in the kitchen last night, sipping her warm milk. Traditional two-piece flannel, pink with a pattern of snowflakes, that covered her more than adequately. (And even that image had driven him out of his mind, leading him to wonder about the soft, feminine curves undoubtedly hidden beneath the shapeless fabric.)

She wasn't covered adequately now.

She was barely covered at all.

For a woman who couldn't be more than five feet four inches, she had some legs beneath the hem of that silky wrap. Long, shapely legs.

"I'm not sure I'd describe what you're wearing as pjs," he remarked, pleased that his voice sounded only slightly strangled.

She paused in front of him, a rosy blush coloring her cheeks. "A gift from your sisters—who didn't pack anything else for me to wear."

As if Nina and Marisa hadn't tortured him enough over the years.

Except that he knew their intentions were good, like Julian and Ruby's had been, because none of them knew that his marriage to Winter wasn't a real marriage.

Of course, the road to hell was paved with good intentions, and looking at Winter now, he felt so hot, he suspected he was already there.

He cleared his throat. "You look…"

"Ridiculous?" she guessed, the color in her cheeks deepening.

He shook his head, unable to answer with anything less than the absolute truth. "Sexy as hell."

"Do you really think so?" she asked.

"How can you doubt it?"

"Because those aren't words I've ever heard used to describe me before."

"And now I have one more reason to hate your ex-husband."

"Don't hate him," Winter urged. "He's not worth the energy."

"We might have to agree to disagree on that one."

She gave him a small smile, then her eyes shifted to the other side of the room. "Is it okay if I get into bed?"

"Oh. Yes. Of course."

She padded in bare feet—toenails painted siren red, he noted. When she reached the bed, she unbelted and removed the silky wrap to reveal a barely there chemise with tiny straps, a low-cut bodice that did little to contain her spectacular breasts and a short flowy skirt that just covered her bottom.

He could hear the flames of the underworld crackling, feel the heat burn his flesh, making his blood pulse hotly in his veins.

Apparently oblivious to his torturous state of enrapture, Winter pulled back the covers, sending the rose petals flying through the air.

"*Dios.*" She dropped to her knees and began scooping up the scattered flowers.

He was immediately beside her, unfurling her hands to release the petals she'd gathered. "Don't worry about those."

"I'm sorry." She wouldn't meet his gaze. "I've made such a mess."

He put a finger under her chin and gently tipped her head up. "There's no reason for you to apologize. You didn't make a mess."

She looked at the carpet. "This is a mess."

"But you're not responsible. Whoever put the flowers on the bed is responsible." He picked up a single petal and rubbed it between his fingers. "Roses," he realized. "I'm sorry. Ruby wouldn't have had any way to know that you hate roses."

"It's okay," she said. "Petals don't seem to have the same impact as blossoms on long stems."

"Well, that's good." He was suddenly aware that they were both kneeling on the carpet, facing one another.

And while he was still fully dressed in his wedding attire, she was wearing next to nothing, and that low-cut bodice did nothing to impede his view of her gloriously full breasts, the nipples drawn into tight peaks now straining against the practically sheer fabric.

He quickly stood up and offered a hand.

Though she let him help her to her feet, he noticed that her cheeks were flushed and she was still having trouble meeting his gaze.

No doubt she'd caught him ogling her like a teenage boy seeing female breasts for the first time. And though he had seen plenty of breasts since that initial glimpse so many years ago, it was his first glimpse of Winter's breasts—and they were truly spectacular.

And definitely not something he should be thinking of now, he realized, aware that the blood that should be pumping through his veins was instead pooling in his groin. Again.

"Get into bed," he said.

She sucked in a breath, obviously startled by his harsh tone. "You're angry with me."

He shook his head. "No."

"You sound angry."

"I'm not angry. I'm…frustrated," he admitted.

"With me," she guessed.

"With the situation."

"A situation I created."

"A situation my brother and sister-in-law created."

A tiny furrow appeared between her brows. "I think we might be talking about different situations."

"Quite possibly," he acknowledged.

"I thought you were angry—or frustrated—because you suddenly realized that you're stuck married to me."

"I made my vows willingly," he assured her.

"Then why are you frustrated?"

Did she really not understand?

Was he going to have to spell it out to her?

"Because we're two people stuck together in a room with only one bed."

"Oh."

He nodded grimly.

"But…we *are* married."

"That's what the minister said," he agreed.

"So if you wanted to...consummate our marriage..."

Her cheeks were nearly as red as her toenails now.

"...I—I wouldn't mind," she finished in a rush.

"You wouldn't mind?" he echoed.

"I mean...if you want me... I want to be with you," she said. "I owe you that much."

Her quiet statement, earnestly spoken, squeezed his heart.

"Winter, *cariño*, you don't owe me anything."

"I owe you *everything*."

And God help him, he was so hard for her now, he was perilously close to snatching up what she was offering with both hands.

He took a deliberate step back, away from her, instead.

"Get into bed," he said, more gently this time.

She quickly scrambled under the covers and pulled them up to her chin, and he managed to exhale a quiet sigh of relief that her far too tempting body was no longer on display.

Unfortunately, he couldn't unsee what he'd seen. And he couldn't stop the throbbing in his veins. But he could remove himself from the temptation, so that's what he did.

He escaped into the bathroom and under the spray of a very cold shower.

After he'd scrubbed his body dry, he looked in the bag his brothers had packed for him and found himself facing a similar dilemma. Obviously Julian and Diego hadn't anticipated that he'd need pajamas, so they hadn't packed him any. Apparently he was going to have to sleep in a T-shirt and his boxer briefs, which would do nothing to hide his body's physical response to her nearness. And not even a king-size bed provided enough distance between them for him to trust that he wouldn't respond to her nearness.

But he spent enough time in the bathroom that, by the time he came out, Winter was sleeping—or at least pretending to be.

***

"Welcome home," Luca said the next day, as he ushered his bride to the front door of the single story cabin that was their new home. "It's small, but it should serve the purpose for now."

"It's perfect," Winter said, stepping over the threshold.

When she'd agreed to marry Luca, she'd assumed they'd end up renting a place in town, though she knew doing so meant her husband would have to leave before the sun was up to get to his ranch job on time. But apparently, in addition to a sizeable bunkhouse, the owner of Cedar Ridge Ranch had several cabins on the property that he made available to his married hands—including the one in which Will and Nicole lived and where Luca and his siblings had grown up. She could tell from the outside that this one was quite a bit smaller than his parents' place, but undoubtedly big enough for the two of them—though they'd be three before the summer.

Most important, though, it was theirs.

Hers and Luca's.

She would be safe here.

And so would their baby.

"I wasn't sure about the decor," Luca admitted. "But Mr. Miller assured me that you could change anything you didn't like. Rearrange the furniture, change the paint, paper the walls."

She made a face then. "I can assure you, I have no intention of putting up wallpaper."

"Which means I won't have to help put up wallpaper, so thank you for that."

"You're welcome."

"The kitchen's a little dated, but the appliances are all in working order—including the washer and dryer in the mudroom."

"I thought for sure I'd have to haul baskets of dirty clothes to the laundromat in town."

"This place doesn't have a lot of perks," he told her. "But laundry facilities is one."

"A big one," she agreed.

"Unfortunately there's only one bedroom and one bed," he said.

"Déjà vu," she murmured.

"Obviously you'll sleep there and I'll sleep on the sofa."

She frowned. "Why is that obvious?"

"Because you're pregnant."

"And the sofa is more my size than yours," she pointed out.

"I'll manage."

"You shouldn't have to manage."

"I'm willing to compromise on a lot of things," Luca said. "But this isn't one of them. You'll sleep in the bed—that's not up for debate."

And for some inexplicable reason, her eyes filled.

Which made him feel like slime.

"I'm sorry," he immediately apologized. "We can debate if you want to."

She managed to smile through her tears. "Why are you so good to me?"

"I'm your husband," he reminded her. "I took a vow to cherish you."

He'd also vowed to love her, and though she had no intention of reminding him of that now, she wondered if he might ever grow to care so deeply for her. But wondering and wishing served no purpose, so she reminded herself to be grateful for what she had, which was so much more than she'd envisioned when she'd been staring at the results of her pregnancy test five days earlier.

Chapter Eight

Their honeymoon was over the next day.

Literally.

Winter, awakened by Luca banging around in the kitchen, opened her eyes to discover that the room was pitch-black. A glance at the clock on the bedside table told her why—it wasn't yet 6:00 a.m.

Still practically the middle of the night, in her opinion.

But ranch work started early, and as the wife of a ranch hand now, she realized that she needed to do the same.

After a quick pit stop in the bathroom, she made her way to the kitchen.

"I didn't mean to wake you," Luca apologized.

"I should be up, anyway," she said.

"Why?"

"To make you breakfast? Or at least smile at you across the table? Wasn't that one of the sweet surprises you were looking for in a marriage?"

"It was a suggestion, not a requirement," he told her. "And I was thinking of the days when we both got to sleep in. I don't expect you to get up before the sun just because I have to."

"Oh."

"But I appreciate the thought."

"Well, I'm up now," she said. "So I could scramble some eggs."

"I like scrambled eggs."

And so began the morning routine of their married life.

And since she'd gotten such an early start and really didn't have much else to do, she decided to head into town and catch up on the bookkeeping she'd let slide the previous week while she was busy preparing for her wedding.

She'd been at her desk less than an hour when Dominic knocked on the door and announced, "Someone's here to see you."

Winter finished recording the numbers she'd calculated in the spreadsheet before she glanced away from the computer screen. "Who is it?"

He shrugged. "She didn't say. She just asked to see you."

The "she" ruled out the possibility that it might be Luca, which was disappointing.

On the other hand, it also ruled out the possibility that it might be Matt, which was a relief. Not that she had any reason to believe he would show up in Tenacity looking for her now, but ever since the word "pregnant" appeared on her pregnancy test, she'd been a little paranoid that he might somehow find out about the baby and come looking for her.

"This is a surprise," Winter said, greeting her mom with a warm hug.

"We stopped by the cabin—Luca gave us the address," she explained. "But no one was there."

"I would have been, if I'd known you were planning to visit," she said.

"We didn't think to call ahead. We didn't expect that you'd be back at work already," Josefina said.

"Dad's with you?"

"Of course. Pablo dragged him into the back to sample something he's been working on."

"Black bean taquitos," Winter guessed. "They're not new on the menu, but he's tweaked the recipe. And they're delicious."

"It's Sunday. And not even forty-eight hours after your wedding. Why are you here?" Josefina demanded, when her daughter failed to respond to her earlier comment.

"Mr. Castillo pretty much lets me make my own hours, so long as the work gets done, and since Luca had to be at the ranch today, I figured I might as well come here."

"How long do you plan on working?"

"My hours are flexible," Winter said. "I can finish now and have lunch with you, if you don't have other plans."

"That would be nice," her mom agreed. "But I wasn't asking about your schedule today but how long you plan to continue working."

"I'm not sure I understand the question," she said cautiously.

"You're married now and you're going to have a baby in six months."

Winter ignored the guilt that tugged in her belly.

She hated lying to her parents, but in this instance, there hadn't been any other choice. She'd had to shift her due date when she told her parents she was pregnant so they would believe Luca was the father of her baby. If they knew she was due in May rather than June, they'd surmise—correctly—that Winter had already been pregnant when she came to Tenacity.

"I'm aware, *Má*," she finally responded.

"You can't continue to prioritize your career over your marriage."

"I've been married two days."

"And already you're back at work. You didn't even take time for a proper honeymoon."

"As you're aware, our plans for the wedding came together rather quickly. There wasn't time to book a proper honeymoon."

"I'm aware," her mother agreed grimly. "But I wasn't only talking about this marriage."

Winter stiffened at that, but Josefina forged ahead anyway, either not noticing her daughter's reaction or not caring.

"If you'd made sure Matt knew he was more important than your work, you might still be married."

"I don't want to talk about Matt," she said firmly.

"I know he encouraged you to stay home, so that you could start a family, and you refused. Now you're starting a family with Luca but still refusing to stay home."

"Do you know why Matt wanted me to stay home, *Má*?" she said. "So that no one would see the bruises he left when he grabbed me and squeezed too tight."

Josefina gasped. "No. Tell me that's not true."

Winter sighed wearily. "Do you really think I'd make up something like that?"

"Matt loved you," her mother said, apparently needing to believe it.

"Matt did a good job acting like he loved me when we were around other people—and an even better job making me feel unworthy when we were alone."

Josefina seemed troubled by this concise summary of the situation—or maybe she was still unconvinced.

"I know you don't want to think poorly of him," Winter said. "And that you can't imagine him doing the things I've told you he did. In the beginning, I couldn't imagine them, either, because the things he said and did were outside my realm of experience. I even tried to convince myself that I'd misunderstood his words or misinterpreted his actions, because that seemed more tolerable than believing that the man I'd fallen in love with didn't really exist.

"But I'm not making this up. And I would never have walked out on my marriage, disregarding the vows I'd made, if he hadn't broken those vows—every single one of them—first."

"Nobody is perfect," Josefina said. "Everyone makes mistakes, and a marriage requires understanding and forgiveness."

"Doesn't a marriage also require respect and caring?"

"Well, of course."

"And am I supposed to believe that Matt respected me when he slept with other women? Was he showing that he cared about me when he called me stupid or lazy?"

The furrow in her mother's brow deepened.

"I'm not asking you to approve of my decision to end my marriage," Winter said. "I'm not even asking you to understand. But I am asking you to respect and accept that I have moved on with my life, with Luca."

"Everything has happened so fast... I will try," Josefina said. "But I think it might take some time for me to reconcile what you have told me about Matt with the man I thought I knew."

"It took me some time, too," Winter acknowledged, relieved that her mom was finally starting to understand not just her reasons for, but the necessity of, her divorce. "But denial was dangerous in my situation."

Josefina considered that for a moment before she asked, "You're not concerned that you don't know Luca any better than you knew Matt?"

"No," she said sincerely. "Luca is a good man. Maybe the best man—aside from *Papá*—I've ever known.

"After Matt, I didn't think I'd find a good man. I wasn't looking for another man. But even when I wasn't looking, he was there."

"He is good to you?"

She nodded, happy to be able to reassure her mother. "Very good."

"And you love him?"

Winter nodded again, because she knew it was the expected response. The answer that would help Josefina accept Winter and Luca's marriage.

And if she felt a little bit guilty about lying to her mother, well, she'd already lied about so many other things she didn't think one more really mattered.

But even as she justified the falsehood in her mind, in a tiny corner of her heart, she suspected that this one more lie might actually be the truth.

Luca sniffed the air as he removed his coat and boots inside the door. "Mmm...something smells good."

"That would be your mother's pozole," Winter said from the kitchen.

"One of my favorites," he noted.

"So she mentioned, when she dropped it off earlier."

"Do you not like pozole?" he asked.

"I like it just fine," she assured him.

"Then why are you trying to kill that cabbage?" he asked warily, as she brought the knife down—hard—again.

"I don't know." She scraped the chopped leaves off the board and into a bowl.

"You're upset about something," he said.

"No, I'm not," she denied. Then she sighed. "Or maybe I am. But I shouldn't be. It's ridiculous to feel annoyed that I haven't had to cook a meal since we've been married."

"We've only been married five days," he pointed out.

"I know. And we've got enough meals in the freezer for five weeks."

"I'm sure that's an exaggeration."

She slid him a look.

"Not the point," he realized.

"It's not that I don't appreciate your mom's generosity," she said. "Because I do. And apparently the birria and tamales and enchiladas and pozole are all your favorites."

"I think I'm still missing the point."

"I'm your wife—and I don't even know what your favorites are."

"We've only been married five days," he said again.

"I do know how to cook," she pointed out to him.

"I'm sure you do."

"In fact, Rafael and Sera said that my Chicken Florentine was the best they'd ever tasted."

"I hope you'll make it for me some time," Luca told her.

"I'd be happy to," Winter said. "But first we have to eat all the meals we've got in the freezer."

"Why?"

She frowned. "What do you mean, *why*?"

"I mean, if you want to make Chicken Florentine, make Chicken Florentine. If you want to make spaghetti and meatballs, make spaghetti and meatballs. And if you don't want to make anything, don't make anything."

"I can't not make anything," she said. "We have to eat."

"But it's not your job to cook for me, and I definitely don't want you stressing over what you want to be cooking."

"I know it's not my job," she acknowledged. "But what is?"

He eyed her warily. "What do you mean?"

"I'm your wife, Luca."

"I'm aware," he assured her.

"As you pointed out, we've been married five days. When we're in public, we hold hands and sit close, playing the part of happy newlyweds. But when we come home, you keep a ten-foot distance between us at all times."

He glanced pointedly across the counter. "This kitchen isn't even ten feet wide."

"Okay, six feet," she amended.

"I don't want you to feel…crowded."

"Is that really the reason—or is it that *you* don't want to feel crowded?"

"I grew up with two brothers and two sisters," he reminded her. "I don't have a problem with being crowded."

"Do you have a problem with me?"

"No, I don't have a problem with you, either."

"Not exactly words to melt a woman's heart," she remarked.

"What do you want me to say?" he asked, feeling at a loss.

She shook her head. "Nothing."

But he suspected her *nothing* really meant *something*.

Unfortunately, he didn't have a clue what that *something* was.

"You're late," Winter said, when Luca came in for dinner the following night.

As soon as the words were out of her mouth, she wished she could take them back. She knew better than to chastise her husband or comment on his schedule, and she immediately braced herself for his explosive response.

But Luca wasn't Matt, a fact she was reminded of when he responded to her untraditional greeting with an apology.

"Sorry," he said. "I should have let you know that I was making a detour to Mustang Pass on the way home."

"That's quite a detour," she noted.

"There's a bigger grocery store there, and I wanted to bring home dessert. Or maybe it's a peace offering," he acknowledged, handing her the tub of ice cream.

Her face lit up when she looked at the label. "Black cherry with dark chocolate chunks!"

"You said it was your favorite."

"You went all the way to Mustang Pass to get ice cream for me?"

"It's not all that far."

"A peace offering, you said."

He shrugged.

"Are we at war?"

"You seemed pretty mad at me last night."

"I was mad at you," she confided. "And even more mad at the situation."

"I don't like when you're mad at me."

"Sometimes mad is necessary," she said. "Or at least safer than the alternative."

"What was your alternative?" he asked curiously.

She recalled her impulse to throw herself at him and kiss him senseless. To press her body against his in an effort to elicit some kind of reaction.

Thankfully, she'd managed to tamp down on that impulse and spare herself further embarrassment, and she had no intention of sharing that foolhardy plan with him now.

Instead, she touched her lips to his cheek and said, "Thank you for the ice cream."

Luca still wasn't entirely sure what he'd done to upset Winter, but at least she'd seemed pleased with his peace offering and willing to forgive and forget. And over the next couple of days, they settled into something of a routine, though he sometimes felt as if they were playing house, knowing that their marriage was nothing more than a formality. A piece of paper to legitimize their relationship so that he could be named on her child's birth certificate.

So while the other ranch hands teased him about being in a hurry to get home to his lovely bride, the truth was, Luca wouldn't have minded working longer hours, because it was torture being with Winter and not being able to touch her and kiss her and strip her naked and spend hours making love with her.

But he'd known what the deal was when they got married, and it didn't include his bride sacrificing herself to satisfy his prurient desires in exchange for him giving her baby his name.

Sometimes when he got home, though, exhausted from the physical labor of the day, she'd look so damn happy to see him that he forgot he was worn out and felt instead as if he was the luckiest man alive just because she was smiling at him.

Which was what happened on Friday—their one-week anniversary. He found himself so enraptured by her happy smile that it took him a minute to notice that she'd rearranged the living room furniture and another minute to pick up on the earthy fragrance of fresh pine that scented the air.

"You got a Christmas tree," he noted.

She nodded, that radiant smile illuminating her face and brightening the whole cabin. "I hope you don't mind," she said. "But I was feeling the holiday spirit."

"Of course, I don't mind," he told her, his own lips curving as he plucked a couple of pine needles from her hair. "This is your home—you should feel free to do whatever you want. But I am wondering where you got the tree. And how you managed to get it set up in here. And who moved the furniture, because that's not something you should be doing in your condition."

"I got the tree at Hendrick's Farm. They strapped it onto the roof of my SUV and when I got home, I called Rafael to get it down and help me wrestle it into the stand."

"I would have been happy to help, if you'd waited for me."

"I was torn between waiting for you, so we could pick out our first Christmas tree together, and getting it myself so that I could surprise you," she confided. "As you can see, wanting to surprise you won out."

"You succeeded," he said.

"It was only after the tree was already up that I remembered you saying you don't like surprises," she admitted, a little sheepishly.

"Some surprises—like this one—are good surprises."

Her smile lit up again.

"And the best is yet to come." She bent over to plug the extension cord into the light socket.

Suddenly the tree was illuminated with hundreds of multicolored lights.

"Wow."

"Some people just drape the lights over the ends of the branches, but I like to weave them up and down, so the lights shine from within."

"There are so many lights, I almost feel like it doesn't need anything else."

"Nice try," she said. "But it still needs ornaments and candy canes and an angel."

"Do you have all of those things?" he asked her.

"Everything except the candy canes," she confirmed. "I'll get those when I'm in town tomorrow."

"Where'd you get the other stuff?"

"Your mom. She claimed she's acquired so many ornaments over the years, she could easily decorate two or three trees, but since they only have room for one, she was happy to share."

"So when do you plan to finish decorating?"

"I was hoping we could do that part together. Maybe after dinner," she said, then closed her eyes and muttered a curse. *"Dios, soy tan estúpido."*

"Hey," Luca protested. "I don't want to hear you say things like that."

"I'm sorry. I was so focused on the tree, I completely forgot about dinner. And you've been working outdoors all day—you're probably starving."

"I'm not starving," he assured her. "And it's not a big deal if we eat later tonight."

She exhaled a long, unsteady breath. "You really mean that, don't you?"

"I wouldn't say it if I didn't," he assured her.

"I keep forgetting that you don't play those kind of mind games." She started for the kitchen. "Thankfully, we've got a freezer full of casseroles."

"So we'll throw something in the oven and work on the tree until dinner's ready."

Winter was relieved to know that her forgetfulness hadn't ruined the whole evening. Though she was sure Luca had to be hungry—and he did filch a couple of cookies from the jar on the counter to tide him over—he didn't seem particularly bothered about having to wait another couple hours for his meal.

So they worked side-by-side hanging the decorations Nicole had donated to their first Christmas tree. It was only when Luca opened a second box that he paused, a bemused expression on his face.

"Why would she have given you these?" he asked, holding up one of a dozen salt dough ornaments. "They look as if they were made by a five-year-old."

"Because you made them when you were five years old and stuck at home with the chicken pox only weeks before Christmas. And because I loved the idea of hanging them on our tree."

"The idea is great." He scrutinized another one that might have been Santa Claus—or maybe a snowman. "The result—not so much."

She took the ornament from his hand and hung it on the tree.

"And when our kids bring home ornaments that they make at school, we'll add theirs to the tree, too."

"Kids?" he echoed, with a pointed look at the barely visible swell of her belly. "Is there something you haven't told me?"

"As far as I know, there's only one baby in there," she assured him. "Hopefully that will be confirmed at our first ultrasound appointment."

"Fingers crossed," he said.

"But I also hope he or she won't be an only child forever."

Though no one had ever accused him of being overly intuitive, it seemed to Luca that Winter was suggesting they might have a baby of their own someday—a brother or sister for the baby she was carrying now. Which meant that she obviously expected their relationship to…change…in the future. Because making a baby required physical intimacy, and that was something he'd been trying to avoid even thinking about since they exchanged vows—and especially since she'd made it clear that she felt she owed him.

If they ever made love—*por favor, Dios*, let it be *when* rather than *if*—it wouldn't be a transactional relationship but the culmination of a mutual attraction, when he was confident that she wanted him as much as he wanted her.

Until then, he would be patient—no matter how frustrated and uncomfortable that patience made him feel.

He cleared his throat. "Let's see how we manage with one before you start adding to the number," he suggested.

"Sounds reasonable," she agreed, reaching into yet another box to lift out a very old—and again familiar—handmade angel.

"My mother must have dug deep into her Christmas stuff to find that. I didn't even know she still had it." He noted the bent wing and missing eye. "*Why* did she still have it?"

"Because *you* made it."

"I don't think I did."

"You know you did." She nudged him playfully with her elbow. "That's why you're blushing."

"I'm not blushing."

She laughed. "Your face is so red right now."

"It's the reflection of the lights on the tree."

"Apparently Mrs. Hill—your second-grade teacher—always had her students make tree toppers as their holiday art project. Julian's topped the tree for two years until Diego came home with his, and then, two years later, yours dethroned his. Then Mrs. Hill retired, so Nina and Marisa never got to make one, which meant that yours maintained its place of honor for a few more years until Diego asked your mom if she only liked your angel best or if she liked you best, too."

"Sounds like something Diego would say," Luca admitted with a wry smile.

"So your angel came off the top of the tree and she pulled out Julian's and Diego's again and set them, side-by-side, on the windowsill."

He set the angel aside, then took her hands in his, frowning as he examined her chafed fingers and palms. "What happened here?"

"Weaving all those lights through prickly branches takes a toll," she said lightly.

"You should have waited for me to do it."

"I'm not fragile, Luca."

"No, not fragile," he agreed. "But precious."

The simple remark, sincerely spoken, caused an unexpected warmth to bloom inside her chest.

"Are you suggesting that I should leave any tasks that might damage my soft hands for my big, strong husband? Because that probably includes changing diapers."

His gaze narrowed even as his lips twitched. "Nice try."

She shrugged. "I figured it was worth a shot."

"I'm not going to do them all, but I'll do my share," he promised.

"Sounds fair," she said.

In truth, it was more than fair, and she was grateful for his willingness to not only give her baby his name but take a hands-on role in raising their child.

And because thinking about how wonderful he'd been from day one was making her a little emotional, she decided to lighten the mood. "Of course, that's easy to say but hard to do when the baby will be here with me all day while you're out babysitting a bunch of cows."

"Is that what you think I do all day?" he asked, torn between insult and amusement.

"No," she admitted. "But I figured you'd get the gist."

"I got the gist." He lifted her hands in turn and pressed a kiss to each palm.

It was a sweet gesture—and certainly not the kind that should make her heart hammer against her ribs. But her heart apparently didn't get that memo, because hammering it was.

"Kissing my boo-boos to make them better?" she asked.

He shrugged. "It works with Emery."

She glanced at their still joined hands for a moment, then shifted her eyes to meet his again. "And if I said I bit my lip when I was wrestling with the lights?"

His gaze dropped to her mouth. "Then I'd have to kiss that boo-boo, too, wouldn't I?"

"Seems only fair," she agreed.

After an almost imperceptible hesitation, he gently touched his lips to hers. But instead of pulling back, as he'd done when he kissed her palms, he lingered.

"Better?" He whispered the question against her lips.

"Almost. I think another kiss might help."

He complied without any hesitation this time.

And Winter savored the flavor of his kiss, the warmth and strength of the arms that had come around her, the heat and hardness of his body against hers. As his mouth moved over hers, as her mind clouded and her body yearned, she thought that this maybe—*finally*—was a signal he was ready to take their relationship to the next level.

Then the oven buzzed, signaling that dinner was ready, and he lifted his lips from hers and stepped back.

"You go put some cream on those hands," he suggested. "I'll serve up dinner."

Chapter Nine

"I've got a doctor's appointment next Wednesday," Winter told Luca, as they dug into their belated meal.

He paused with his fork halfway to his mouth. "Is everything okay?"

She nodded. "As far as I know. It's my first appointment, after which I'll have regular monthly checkups. That's the norm until the eighth month, when the doctor will likely want weekly exams."

"Should I go with you?"

"Do you want to?"

"Sure." He nodded. "Yeah. I could do that."

"You don't have to, if you don't want to," she told him. "I know you've taken a lot of time off recently. Because of me."

"I want to," he assured her.

"Okay. Because the book I'm reading promotes the involvement of the dad through all stages of the pregnancy, especially if he's going to be present during the delivery."

"Am I going to be present during delivery?" he asked, aware that it was entirely her decision.

"I hope so," she said. "After all, this is your baby, too."

"And I absolutely want to be there when he or she is born, so I'm happy to go to the doctor with you and to prenatal classes. Whatever else you need—I'm in."

"Thank you." She pushed her food around her plate. "You're doing so much for me…and you've been so great about everything…"

"That was the deal," he reminded her.

"But...what are you getting out of this?"

"Are you kidding? I've got a sexy wife who's soon going to have a baby."

"Not very soon," she said. "We've still got another almost five months. And obviously you don't really think I'm sexy or..."

"Or what?" he prompted, when her words trailed off again.

She only shook her head, but he could see the shimmer of tears in her eyes.

Dios—what had he said or done to make her cry?

"*Cariño.*" He reached across the table to touch her hand. "What's wrong?"

"It's just... Nothing." She sniffled. "Hormones."

Then she abruptly pushed her chair away from the table and made her escape.

"Do you want to watch a movie?" Luca asked, after the kitchen had been tidied up and the dishes cleaned and put away.

Since her meltdown at dinner, he'd been tiptoeing around her but thankfully hadn't pressed for any more of an explanation. Or maybe "hormones" was all the explanation a pregnant woman required.

"What kind of movie?" Winter wondered, trying not to sound too eager.

She usually enjoyed reading before bed, but she'd already gone through three novels in the week since their wedding, trying to stay out of Luca's way as he'd obviously been making an effort to stay out of hers.

"Your choice," he said.

"Really?"

"Sure."

"Even if I choose a Christmas movie?"

"'Tis the season," he noted.

"Even if it's a romantic Christmas movie?" she pressed.

To his credit, he managed not to wince.

"Your choice," he said again. "And while you figure out what we're going to watch, I'm going to make popcorn."

"We just finished dinner."

"So?"

"So... I wouldn't think you'd be hungry so soon after dinner."

"You don't have popcorn because you're hungry," he told her. "You have popcorn because it goes with movies—like peanut butter goes with jelly."

"It's hard to argue with that logic," she noted.

"Do you want butter?"

"Thanks, but I don't want any popcorn."

"And yet, your hand will find its way into the bowl when I sit down beside you," he surmised.

She was so intrigued by his offhand mention of sitting beside her that it took a minute for her to respond to his remark. "Why would you assume that?"

"Two sisters," he reminded her. "So...butter or no?"

"Butter," Winter said, far more tempted by the idea of Luca sitting beside her than the prospect of sharing his snack.

While he popped the corn, she changed out of her leggings and sweater and into her favorite pair of flannel pjs—perfect for snuggling up in front of the TV, then she set out drinks and napkins and cued up the movie.

She chose *The Holiday*, a modern classic, in her opinion, and one that she could watch over and over again. When Luca joined her in the living room, he turned off the lamps, so the only illumination came from the television screen and the lights on the Christmas tree.

He sat beside her on the sofa—with the bowl of popcorn between them like a salty chaperone. But at least he wasn't sitting on the opposite side of the room tonight, as he usually did if they were watching TV together.

Though she tried to resist the temptation of the fluffy, buttery popcorn, her hand did find its way to the bowl, just as he'd anticipated. And sometimes, when they reached in at the same moment, their fingers touched.

Just that casual, accidental contact was enough to send tingles of awareness skating through her veins. Luca, in contrast, appeared unaffected. And it was an increasing source of frustration to Winter that while her attraction to him continued to grow, he remained oblivious.

When the popcorn was gone, she set the bowl on the table, eliminating the barrier between them before shifting closer to him. She felt him stiffen when her thigh brushed against his, and happily interpreted his reaction as evidence that perhaps he wasn't as immune to her nearness as he wanted her to believe.

She knew he thought he was being respectful in giving her space, but what she really wanted was for him to invade her space. So far, he'd stubbornly resisted doing so, leading Winter to suspect she was going to have to take matters into her own hands.

On the screen, Arthur—an award-winning screen writer from the Golden Age of Hollywood—was talking to his new neighbor, explaining the difference between leading ladies and best friends in movies, and chastising her for behaving like a best friend when she was meant to be a leading lady.

Winter didn't know if she was meant to be a leading lady, but she wanted to be. She wanted to be the driving force in her own life—someone who didn't just let things happen to her but made them happen.

She continued to mull over that thought as the movie played out on the screen…

The next thing she knew, she was being lifted into a pair of strong arms.

"The movie's not over," she protested sleepily, though she wasn't one hundred percent certain it was true.

"How would you know?" Luca asked, the question tinged with amusement. "You were sleeping."

"I want to see the end," she said, though at the moment, she was enjoying being cradled against his hard chest and carried to bed like the leading lady in a romantic movie.

Unfortunately, like too many sweet holiday films, she suspected the scene would cut there.

"Because you don't know how it ends?" he asked dryly.

"Because I want to see the happy ending."

"That's the great thing about streaming—we can pick it up again where we left off—or where you fell asleep—to see the happy ending tomorrow night. Or the next night," he said, setting her on her feet beside the bed to pull back the covers.

She hesitated when he gestured for her to climb in. "I need to brush my teeth."

"Go ahead."

"Are you going to wait to tuck me in?" she asked hopefully.

"I'll wait," he agreed.

She hurried to the bathroom to complete her usual pre-bedtime routine. And, after a quick check in the mirror, she decided it couldn't hurt to unfasten the top button of her pajama top.

Luca didn't give her—or her exposed cleavage—a second glance when she returned to the bedroom. He just lifted the covers again so that she could slide beneath them.

"You know, despite my growing belly, I don't take up a lot of room in this bed," she told him.

"It's hard to even tell that your belly's growing under all those big sweaters you usually wear," he said.

Completely missing the point, she mused, with no small amount of frustration.

"What I'm trying to say is that the bed is plenty big enough for two people. You could sleep here, too, instead of on that lumpy sofa."

"The sofa's not so bad."

Still missing the point.

He tucked the covers around her and touched his lips to her forehead. "Sweet dreams, Winter."

Then he turned and left the room, confirming that she was married to the most obtuse man in Montana.

After saying good-night to his wife, Luca took himself back to the living room and the admittedly lumpy sofa that did double duty as his bed. As he tossed and turned, he wondered if he truly was a masochist—why else would he have lifted her into his arms and carried her to her bed? Let himself feel her soft curves against his body, driving him into such a state it took every ounce of his willpower to leave her alone in her warm bed and retreat to the cold and empty sofa?

What he should have done, what any other man who wanted to avoid temptation would have done, was nudge her awake so that she could make her own way to bed. But she'd obviously been exhausted, and he'd trusted that he could get her there without awakening her.

A serious miscalculation on his part.

Not only had she woken up, she'd offered to share her bed.

It wasn't the first time she'd hinted at a willingness to share her personal space, and each time, he found it harder and harder to say no—and wondering why the hell he felt compelled to deprive himself of what he really wanted?

Luca had expected marriage would be an adjustment, but he hadn't expected it to be a daily struggle.

What he struggled with most, what he'd been completely unprepared for, was the way his blood stirred when he was near Winter, evidence of his growing attraction to his bride. An attraction he was doing his damnedest to ignore.

The sole reason he'd offered to marry her was so that she could put his name on her baby's certificate and lessen the likelihood that her scumbag ex-husband would be able to lay claim to the child. He hadn't considered that it might be a challenge to live under the same roof, pretending to the world—or at least their families and friends in Tenacity—that they were happily married when the truth was that their marriage was in name only.

But he was dealing with it, and proud of himself for managing to carry on a casual conversation across the dinner table when all he could think about was how much he wanted to kiss her again. How much he longed to feel the press of her soft body against his.

He tried to remember that he'd known her since she was a kid—a friend of Nina and Marisa's. But the woman he'd married bore little resemblance to the girl who used to hang around with his sisters.

She'd been skinny back then, her figure almost boyish. Pretty, though, he acknowledged, with her big eyes and sweet smile. But too young and definitely too innocent for him to pay her any notice.

He was noticing her now, though.

And her previously subtle curves seemed to have been enhanced by her pregnancy. Though he knew she tried to disguise her still subtle baby bump when she went into town, not wanting the world—or at least the rest of Tenacity—to know about her pregnancy just yet, he couldn't deny that he found her new shape incredibly appealing

He didn't know if it was true that all pregnant women were sexy, but there was no denying that descriptor fit his expectant bride. And when he was near her, he found himself feeling all kinds of things he knew he shouldn't be feeling, wanting all kinds of things that he knew he couldn't have.

At the top of the list was an almost desperate desire for the woman he'd married.

The woman who'd offered herself to him like a virgin sacrifice on their wedding night. A virgin sacrifice in sinfully seductive white satin and lace—an image that seemed to be burned into his brain despite his best efforts to scrub it from his memory.

Equally clear, though, were the words she'd spoken.

...if you want me... I want to be with you. I owe you that much.

And that was why, no matter how much he wanted her, he couldn't give in to his desire. Because to do so would be to cross a line that he'd promised himself he would not cross.

It was also why, when he fell into his makeshift bed, physically and mentally exhausted from the physical labors of the day and the even more challenging task of keeping his hands off her, sleep did not come easily. Because he couldn't stop thinking about her and aching for her.

But tonight, when he finally did drift off, Luca let her come to him in dreams in ways he only wished she might in reality.

Despite her mother's ominous warnings about prioritizing her career over her marriage, Winter drove into town the following Monday morning feeling nothing but grateful that she had a job to go to so she wouldn't be stuck in the cabin all day thinking about her husband.

They'd been married over a week, and the only time he'd even kissed her since their wedding day was when she'd tricked him into doing so. And though she knew she had so much to be grateful for—and she was—with each day that passed, she was growing more and more frustrated with the status quo in their marriage.

Unfortunately, there was no one she could talk to about her feelings, because no one—aside from Luca—knew the truth about their marriage and her baby. There was no one she could confide in about her growing feelings for the man who was her husband, but only in the legal sense.

Most of her friends in Butte were also friends—or at least acquaintances—of her ex-husband, too, and she had no intention of telling any of them that she'd married again, never mind share the lack of intimate details of her recent marriage. Not even Alice, her closest friend and former neighbor in Silver Bow County, knew that she was pregnant. Because while Winter knew Alice would never intentionally betray a confidence, she worried that her friend might let the detail slip in casual conversation with Matt.

She briefly considered talking to Bethany, who had proven to be a reliable sounding board and adviser on so many occasions over the years, but it wasn't the kind of conversation she felt comfortable having long distance. All of which left Winter married to a man who didn't want to be with her and so isolated and alone that she couldn't confide in anyone about her conflicted feelings.

Except that she wasn't really alone—not anymore.

There was a tiny life growing inside her and, whatever happened or didn't happen with Luca, that tiny life meant she wouldn't ever be alone again.

A knock on the partially open door interrupted her musings.

She hastily swiped at the tears that had spilled onto her cheeks. "Come in."

The door swung wider and Sera stepped through the opening, an overstuffed bag clenched in her fist.

"My old maternity clothes," she said. "I intended to take them to the church's donation box but never got around to it. Anything you want is yours, anything you don't can go there."

"Thank you," Winter said sincerely. "So far I've managed okay, but even my stretchiest leggings are soon going to run out of stretch."

Sera dropped the bag in the corner then pulled a second chair close to Winter's desk and lowered herself into it.

"I hope you don't mind me saying so, but you don't look like a bride in the honeymoon stages of her marriage," her cousin's wife said gently.

"Being married is a bigger adjustment than I anticipated,"

Winter hedged. "On top of that, the pregnancy hormones are wreaking havoc on my system."

"Been there, cried about everything," Sera confirmed.

"And my parents are back in Texas."

"All good reasons for tears," the other woman agreed. "But I still think there's something more going on here."

"Because that isn't enough?" she asked lightly, unable to disagree with Sera's assessment.

"For most women, sure. But I think you're tougher than that."

"But not nearly as tough as I wish I could be."

Sera glanced at her watch. "Can you take time for a cup of tea?"

"Sure," Winter agreed. "But I'm not the one who has three kids to chase after."

Her cousin's wife winked. "Not yet, anyway."

She managed to smile at that, though the thought of having more babies—Luca's babies—made her heart ache with longing.

"Grab your coat," Sera urged. "We'll take a walk over to the Silver Spur."

It was a short walk to the café, and quiet when they arrived at the restaurant as most of the breakfast crowd had departed and the lunch rush had yet to begin.

Winter ordered a peppermint tea, black, and Sera opted for yerba mate with lots of milk and sugar.

"Do you want anything to snack on?" the server asked. "Our baker's just putting the finishing touches on a fresh batch of sugar cookies."

"The ones shaped like snowflakes?" Sera asked.

"We've got snowmen and Christmas trees today."

Sera looked at Winter.

"Why not?" she decided.

Her friend's grin signaled her approval. "We'll take one of each."

"Good call on the cookies," Winter said, when they were seated at a table by the window.

"We picked up a dozen after church—there were snowflakes yesterday—and they were gone by last night," Sera admitted.

Winter popped the snowman's scarf—decorated with colored sugar—into her mouth. "I could eat a dozen of these myself."

"Well, you are eating for two."

"But one of those two apparently only requires 340 calories a day."

"I won't tell if you don't," her cousin's wife said with a wink.

She laughed, grateful to her friend for helping her shake off her earlier mood.

"I'm glad you could take some time this morning. I've been missing you like crazy since you moved out."

"You have? Really?"

"Really," Sera confirmed. "My husband and kids keep me busy, but it was having you to talk to at the end of the day that kept me sane."

Winter managed to smile at that.

"And if you want to talk…if there was anything you wanted to tell me—anything at all—it wouldn't go any farther," her friend promised. "I'm not a priest bound by the rules of the confessional, but I know how to keep a secret."

"I was actually just lamenting the fact that there was no one in Tenacity that I could confide in," Winter admitted.

"And here I am, happy to be your confidante," Sera said. "But no pressure, if you're not sure—"

"Luca's-not-the-father-of-my-baby."

Sera's mouth fell open in response to the blurted confession.

"Then who—no." She cut herself off. "It's none of my business. I'm here to listen, not question, and definitely not judge."

"Matt," Winter said, answering the aborted question anyway.

The other woman scowled. "That slimy bastard?"

"Unfortunately, yes."

"Does Luca know?" Sera asked cautiously.

Winter nodded.

"Is that why you were upset? Did you fight about it?"

"No." Now she shook her head. "Luca has always known the truth."

Her friend's brows lifted. "Even when he asked you to marry him?"

"Even then," she confirmed.

"Then why— Again, not my business," Sera said, cutting herself off again.

"If I want to be able to talk to you—and I do—you need to be able to ask questions."

"Okay," the other woman agreed.

"You were going to ask why he married me," Winter guessed.

"Actually, I'm pretty sure I can guess why he married you. According to Rafael, Luca's always had his eye on you, even way back when."

"Rafael's wrong," she said.

"I would never say this to his face," Sera confided. "But my husband is rarely wrong."

"Mistaken then," Winter amended.

"I wouldn't bet on that, either," her friend said. "But what I was going to ask was, why did *you* marry Luca?"

"Because I wanted my baby to have a father."

"Your ex didn't want kids?"

"My ex shouldn't ever have kids," Winter responded bluntly. "He's not a good man, he wasn't a good husband and he wouldn't be a good father."

Sera sipped her tea.

"Don't hold back now," Winter told her, surmising that the other woman had purposely occupied her mouth so she couldn't speak.

"I was just wondering...but didn't want to ask...did he... hit you?"

"Only once." And yet the shame of that memory made her cheeks burn.

"That's when you left," Sera guessed.

Winter nodded.

"Usually hitting is an escalation of abuse," her friend noted. "And sometimes the earlier abuse is so subtle, you don't realize it's abuse."

"That about sums it up," she agreed.

"My sister's husband was a bully," Sera confided. "Actually, he's still a bully, but he's no longer her husband. Unfortunately, she still has to communicate and interact with him to accommodate his weekly visitation with their kids."

"Which is what I'm hoping to avoid."

"You're afraid Matt would want access?"

"I'm terrified he'll go after custody," Winter admitted.

"To punish you?" Sera asked. "Or control you?"

"Both are strong possibilities."

"I never did like him," her cousin's wife confided now. "Or maybe it would be more accurate to say that I didn't like the way he talked to you. The way he pretended to be considerate while he was condescending."

"Most people don't see past the facade," Winter said. "I didn't, either, in the beginning."

"Sometimes love truly is blind."

"And maybe I never really loved him at all—because how can you love someone without really knowing him?"

"A good question," Sera noted. "But you know Luca."

She nodded.

"And you love Luca?"

"I'm not entirely sure what my feelings are," she confided. "And I'm even less sure of his."

"Even if he hasn't made any declarations, you have to believe he cares about you deeply. He never would have married you otherwise." Her friend swallowed the last mouthful of her tea. "Unless you seriously rock his world in the bedroom," she suggested as an alternative. "Because men sometimes can't help but think with the wrong parts of their anatomy."

"Then I guess I have to believe he cares about me deeply," Winter said lightly.

Sera winced. "Are you saying the physical part of your relationship isn't great?"

"I'm saying the physical part of our relationship is nonexistent."

"I'm confused," her friend admitted.

"You and me both," Winter confided, staring at the bottom of her now empty cup. "Somehow this is almost more embarrassing to admit than all the other things I've already told you, but…we haven't even consummated our marriage. And not because I don't want to."

Sera's jaw dropped. "Luca's holding out?"

She nodded miserably.

"Does he know you want to?"

"I've dropped some pretty blatant hints."

"Sometimes men need to be hit over the head."

"Is that your advice? Because I'd be lying if I said I wasn't tempted."

Her friend laughed. "I didn't mean literally, though I understand your temptation. There are days I want to smack Rafael several times."

"Do you have any more specific advice to offer?" Winter asked.

"Communicate," Sera said. "It sounds trite, but it really is the key to a successful marriage. Don't hint or imply or suggest—tell him what you want in a way that he can't fail to understand."

She was mulling over her friend's words when the café door opened and an old man in a leather jacket and cowboy hat walked in with an even older woman wearing a puffy red coat and purple cowboy boots.

Winter immediately recognized them as Luca's Great-uncle Stanley and his wife, Winona. While he waited at the counter for whatever they'd ordered, she made her way to the table where Winter and Sera were seated.

"There's the blushing bride," Winona said, addressing Winter before shifting her attention to Sera. "And you look just like Rafael Hernandez's wife, but I don't think I've ever seen her without one or two—or sometimes three—kids tugging at her."

"Sometimes I don't recognize myself without the kids," Sera admitted. "But it's nice, every now and then, to share some one-on-one time with a friend."

"Indeed," Winona agreed, then turned back to Winter. "And how is life as a newlywed?"

"Wonderful," she enthused, with a wide smile that she hoped might give credence to her lie.

The old woman took Winter's hand and cradled it between her own. Her smile faded then and another furrow etched into her deeply wrinkled brow. "Beyond the shadows there is light."

"I'm...sorry?"

"Beyond the shadows there is light," Winona said again.

But hearing the words repeated didn't help Winter make any sense of them.

"You must trust that he will protect and love you...both of you."

Another statement no less baffling than the first, Winter mused.

And before she could figure out how to respond, the old woman gave her hand a gentle squeeze, then moved away to join her husband at a table across the room.

"Is it just me or was that...odd?" Winter asked.

"Very odd," Sera agreed. "But odd is also very typical of Winona."

Chapter Ten

Dr. Carrington, a recent addition to the staff at Bronco Medical, was a fortysomething woman with blunt-cut blond hair, bright blue eyes and a warm smile.

"You must be Winter Sanchez," she said, offering her hand to the expectant mom as soon as she entered the examination room. "I'm Rebecca Carrington."

Winter nodded. "And this is my husband, Luca."

"It's a pleasure to meet you both." The doctor shook Luca's hand in turn, before jumping right into her preliminary questions about the expectant mom's medical history and general health and following up with a basic exam, checking her height, weight and blood pressure.

"We usually do a first ultrasound at around fourteen weeks," the doctor said now. "But mom suspects she's already past that, so we'll take a look at the baby today, get some measurements to see if those jive with her estimate and then figure out the due date. Sound good?"

They both nodded.

The doctor wheeled a portable cart closer to the exam table upon which Winter had been sitting.

"Mom, you can stretch out and make yourself comfortable," she said. "Push your leggings down and pull your sweater up so we can see that beautiful baby belly. Dad, why don't you go around to the other side so you can see what's going on, too?"

While they followed her directions, the doctor tapped her fingers on the keyboard, inputting patient information and exam date.

"Now for the fun part," she said, turning her attention back to the expectant parents. "Getting a first look at your little guy—or girl."

Winter reached for Luca's hand, and he squeezed hers in response, but his gaze was on the screen as the doctor moved the probe over the patient's belly. Her breath caught in her throat as the picture came into focus on the screen, and she squeezed his hand tighter. He didn't make a sound, but he felt something inside his chest, almost as if his heart was actually expanding, filling with love for the tiny being.

"There's our baby," Winter murmured softly, her voice thick with emotion.

"I see him—or her," Luca confirmed, speaking softly as she'd done, affording the moment the reverence it deserved.

"Did you want to know the sex—if baby's willing to show us?"

Winter looked at Luca. "Do we want to know?"

"I'm happy to be surprised," he said. "But it's your call."

"We'll wait," she decided.

The doctor smiled. "It likely would only be a guess at this point, anyway, but no matter how many times I tell that to my patients, the ones who want to know seem personally affronted when later scans or tests—or the unmistakable evidence at birth—proves that initial guess was wrong."

As she chatted with them, she expertly moved the probe with one hand and input numbers—measurements, apparently—into the machine with the other.

"But it looks like you'll only have to wait five months to find out," Dr. Carrington told him. "Your baby is measuring at seventeen weeks, which puts your estimated date of delivery at May 22—pretty close to mom's guess."

Winter looked at him then, and Luca immediately understood the cause for the concern he could see in her eyes.

"Is it true that first babies are always late?" she asked the doctor.

"The words 'never' and 'always' aren't words that should be used to describe any aspect of pregnancy or childbirth, because every expectant mom and every baby is different," Dr. Carrington told them, continuing to tap at the keyboard until the printer connected to the machine began to hum. "But it's not uncommon for first babies to be late—sometimes by as much as two weeks.

"And let me reassure you now, in case your baby doesn't show any signs of wanting to be born even past your EDD—estimated due date—no pregnancy lasts forever." She smiled and handed them a photo of the baby. "And so long as you keep doing all the things you've been doing—eating healthy, getting moderate exercise and taking your prenatal vitamins—you should feel confident that your baby will stay snug and comfortable until he—or she—is ready to be born."

Winter seemed relieved and reassured when they walked out of the doctor's office with the ultrasound picture in her hand.

Our baby, she'd said.

The words had come out of her mouth without hesitation—and so easily that, for just a moment, Luca had almost forgotten that he'd played no part in the creation of the life in her womb.

Over the past ten days, he'd thrown himself so completely into the role of doting husband and expectant father that he'd managed to forget it was only that—a role.

An elaborate deception.

Because when he was with Winter, it felt like so much more.

It felt as deep and real as the feelings he was developing for his wife.

"There's a package for you," Luca said, offering her the box that was propped against the door when they returned from their appointment with Dr. Carrington.

"Sera texted earlier to say something had been delivered

to their house, and she offered to drop it off when she was out running errands."

"Apparently she did."

A few belated gifts had been delivered in the days that had passed since their wedding, but this felt different to Winter. For starters, it was only her name on the label. A label that was obviously computer generated, without any handwriting to trigger the sudden feeling of unease that stirred low in her belly.

But she couldn't deny that something about the package made her uneasy.

"Aren't you going to open it?" Luca asked, when she continued to stare at the box.

"Is it strange that I don't want to?"

"You think it's from Matt," he realized.

"I don't want to think it could be, but I also don't want to take a chance. I don't want anything to spoil this day."

"Nothing is going to spoil this day," Luca promised, and he set the package aside.

But the next day, Winter knew she could ignore the box no longer. And when Luca came home for lunch, he found her sitting at the kitchen table staring at it.

"Do you want me to open it?" he asked her.

She nodded, but then she worried, "Does that make me a coward?"

"No." He crouched in front of her chair. "You are the bravest woman I know—and smart enough to be wary. And since it's not something that you ordered and there's no return address on the package to know where it came from, it's not likely something that you want or need, and we can just toss it in the trash if that makes you feel better."

"I've been sitting here thinking about doing just that," she admitted. "But I think I need to know."

"Okay then." He used his pocketknife to slice through the tape on the box, then opened the flaps to reveal an ornate silver frame inside which was a photo taken on Winter and Matt's wedding day.

A bright pink sticky note stuck to the glass had five words written on it.

Till death do us part

"We should call the police," Luca said.

Winter had to swallow the bile that rose up in her throat before she could respond. "And say what? We have no proof that Matt sent the photo—and that's not even his handwriting on the note."

"Whether we can prove it or not isn't the point. You know he sent it, and you know the words aren't intended as a reminder of your vows but a threat."

She nodded, because she did know.

And while Luca called the police department, the words on the note echoed in her head.

Till death do us part. Matt's gaze had been as hard as his words. Do you remember saying those words, Winter? Do you remember making that vow?

Of course, I remember. She'd managed to respond in an even tone, unwilling to let him know that everything inside her was quivering.

Then why would you ever think that divorce was an option?

Because our marriage isn't working.

A truth that became more and more apparent to her with every passing day.

If it's not, it's because you aren't trying hard enough.

I am *trying, but nothing I do is good enough for you.*

My expectations aren't unreasonable.

And she could tell he honestly believed that.

The problem for Winter was that his expectations were constantly changing, and no matter how hard she tried, her efforts to meet them inevitably fell short.

The first time he'd yelled at her, it was because dinner wasn't *ready to go on the table when he got home. Never mind that she had arrived home only half an hour before he did.*

A few weeks after that, he yelled at her because the chicken she'd put in the oven for dinner was dried out—because he was nearly an hour later than usual arriving home. When she, baffled by his outrage, pointed that fact out to him, he'd grabbed her and shaken her, his fingers digging into the flesh of her upper arms so hard they'd left bruises.

A lousy cook and an insubordinate wife, he'd said, seething, as he dragged her down the hall to the bedroom. Let's see if you can perform at least one wifely duty.

She hadn't tried to fight him off because she knew her efforts would be ineffectual. Instead, she'd lain motionless on the bed and let him do what he wanted.

A subpar performance there, too, he said afterward, shoving her away from him.

"Winter?"

She started at the sound of Luca's voice.

"Honey, you're shaking."

"I'm sorry."

He rubbed his hands briskly up and down her arms, attempting to warm her. "Why are you apologizing?"

"I don't know," she admitted.

"You're not alone, *cariño*. I'm here. Always."

She nodded and clenched her jaw so that he wouldn't realize her teeth were chattering.

"I'm going to take the picture to Chief Everett tomorrow. You can come with me, if you want, or I can file a report on my own, if you don't."

Don't you worry your pretty little head about the details— I'll take care of everything.

"I'll come with you," she said. "Because even more troubling than the photo or the note is the fact that Matt sent the package to Rafael and Sera's address. He knows that I'm in Tenacity."

* * *

For the first few days after filing the report at the police station, it was an effort for Winter to pretend everything was status quo. But with each day that passed without any further word from her ex-husband, she slowly started to relax again. Or maybe it was the fact that Luca made sure she was rarely alone with her thoughts that allowed her to put Matt in the back of her mind and focus on the present.

On the days she wasn't scheduled to work, her husband conscripted members of his family to keep her busy. Which was how she found herself Christmas shopping with Nina and baking cookies with Nicole and helping Marisa design the program for her upcoming holiday pageant. And every night, he snuggled with her on the sofa, watching one or another of her favorite Christmas movies without a word of complaint.

And if it wasn't exactly how Winter had envisioned her life as Luca's wife, she considered herself fortunate to be married to such an attentive and supportive husband. A fact of which she reminded herself every time she crossed paths with Sera and had to respond to her friend's questioning glances with a negative shake of her head.

"We're having chicken tortilla soup tonight," Winter announced from the kitchen when Luca came in after work the following Wednesday.

"Sounds good to me," he said.

"Does it?" she asked sweetly. "Because your mother dropped it off for me, as I'm apparently under the weather."

He didn't look at her as he retrieved two bowls from the cupboard. "Well, it's certainly soup weather."

"Do you have any idea where she might have gotten the impression that I was feeling unwell?" she pressed.

"Not from me," he assured his wife. "I haven't spoken to her in a few days."

"Perhaps from your dad, then?" she suggested. "I understand he had lunch here with you today."

"Yeah, he did."

"Why would you tell him I was sick?" Winter asked, clearly baffled.

"I didn't actually say you were sick," he hedged. "Just that you were a little...congested."

"Congested?" she repeated with a frown.

He sighed. "I needed to explain why you were snoring."

"I do *not* snore," she informed him indignantly.

"But you might, if you were congested," he pointed out. "And that was the first thing that came to mind to explain why I'd slept on the sofa."

She frowned at that. "How did he know you slept on the sofa?"

"Because my pillow and blankets were still there."

"My fault," Winter realized. "Rafael sent me a text message asking if I could pick him up on my way to the restaurant because Sera needed the car, and I hurried off without tidying the living room."

"It's not your job to put my things away. It's mine—and my fault, because usually I don't think about it, which is why you got in the habit of doing so."

"Still." She sniffed. "You might have come up with a better explanation than I was snoring."

"What should I have said?" he challenged. "Should I have told him that I sleep on the sofa because we're married in name only?"

"No," she admitted, the wind taken out of her sails. "But for the record, when you suggested that we get married, you never said that it was going to be a marriage in name only."

He frowned at that. "I assumed it was understood."

"Well, you assumed wrong."

"But..."

She stirred the soup. "Are you going to finish that thought?"

"But you'd just recently escaped from an oppressive marriage, and I know the only reason you accepted my proposal was to minimize the likelihood that your ex-husband might lay claim to your baby."

"No matter how desperate I was to give my baby a father, I wouldn't have married you if I thought you were anything like Matt," she told him.

"Even so, no one would blame you for being a little apprehensive."

"I'm not apprehensive, Luca. And if we want to honor the 'till death do us part' part of our vows, shouldn't we try to make this a real marriage?"

"I know you think you owe me—"

"Because I do."

"But I'm not going to take advantage of your feelings of gratitude."

"Not even if I want you to take advantage?"

He opened his mouth to respond, then closed it again without saying a word.

"Do you have a girlfriend? A lover?" she challenged.

"What? No!" He sounded genuinely affronted by the question. "Of course not."

"Then the problem is that you're just not attracted to me," she concluded unhappily.

"The problem is that I'm doing my damnedest not to let you see how desperately attracted I am to you."

And then, while she stood there, stunned into silence by his unexpected response, he walked out the door.

Chapter Eleven

Luca shouldn't have walked out on her, but he knew that if he hadn't—if he'd stayed... Well, he didn't dare let his mind go down the path of what might have happened, because his body had kept him awake all night, tossing and turning on the damn sofa, aching to realize any one of numerous tempting possibilities.

So on his way home the following day, and despite the fact that they were on a tight schedule because his sister's holiday pageant was that night, he took a quick trip into town.

"Another peace offering?" Winter asked, when he handed her the bouquet of flowers he'd bought—minus the roses he'd plucked out and dropped in the trash.

"An apology," he said. "I shouldn't have walked out on you last night."

"An apology isn't necessary," she said stiffly. "Or, if it is, perhaps I'm the one who should apologize for pushing you in a direction that obviously made you uncomfortable."

"You didn't. I wasn't—" He huffed out a breath and scrubbed his hands over his face. "There were a lot of things we didn't talk about before we got married, and maybe we both made certain—and different—assumptions about those things."

"It seems we did," she agreed.

"So perhaps we should clarify."

"Okay."

"I married you to give your baby a father," he said.

"You were perfectly clear about that," she assured him.

"But that wasn't the only reason. I—I care about you, Winter."

"I know you do," she said, her expression softening a little. "And I care about you, too, which is why I'm going to put this awkward conversation on hold right now so that we have time to get ready and grab dinner before the holiday pageant."

"On hold," he echoed. "Does that mean you're going to want to resume it again later?"

"Most likely," she agreed.

"Great," he said, with obviously feigned cheerfulness. "Something to look forward to."

But at least Winter was smiling as she retreated to the bedroom to get ready.

They were planning to eat at T. Bones tonight—a recent and welcome addition to the short list of Tenacity food venues. The new restaurant had scarred hardwood floors, faux leather banquettes and servers casually dressed in jeans with black T-shirts and red half aprons, but the real draw was that it had already established a reputation for good food and reasonable prices.

By the time Luca had showered and dressed, Winter was waiting at the door, her long coat buttoned and tall boots on her feet, so it wasn't until they got to the restaurant and he helped her remove her outer layer that he discovered what she was wearing beneath.

"Is that a new dress?" he asked, after the server had recited the daily specials and taken their drink orders.

"New to me, anyway," she said. "Sera gave me a bag full of maternity clothes and this was in it."

"It's nice," he said, thinking that the bold red color complimented her complexion almost as much as the fabric did her curves.

"I was concerned that the sweater knit would emphasize my baby bump, but she assured me that until my belly is bigger than my breasts, no one will be looking at my belly."

Luca scowled. "I don't like the idea of other people looking at your...figure."

"I don't know why it would bother you, since you obviously have no interest in looking—or doing anything else."

He held her gaze across the table as he cautioned, "Don't mistake lack of action for lack of interest, *cariño*."

"*Dios*, Luca. You give more mixed signals than a drunk flag person."

"Then I'll apologize for that, too," he said, as the server returned with their beverages and a basket of warm parmesan garlic knots.

Conversation shifted to easier topics then, and after dinner—simple but delicious steaks accompanied by loaded baked potatoes—they made their way to the gymnasium of the high school for the Tenacity Holiday Pageant. Clearly the town's residents expected it to live up to its billing as "a multicultural celebration not to be missed," because it seemed to Winter that every single person who lived in Tenacity was there—and likely many more from outside the town limits, too.

For as long as Winter had known her, Marisa had been driven by music. Even as a child, she'd constantly been humming or singing, and her talent had been evident at an early age. Though her parents hadn't had a lot of disposable income, they'd scrimped and saved wherever possible to ensure she got the lessons she needed. And it had paid off.

Audiences were mesmerized by the quick and graceful movement of Marisa's fingers over the piano keys and enthralled by the sound of her voice, which somehow managed to be sweet and pure or strong and passionate, depending on the mood of the singer as much as the song. And while the holiday concert showcased a lot of local talent, there was no denying that the pageant director was the star.

By the time they left the school, after congratulating Marisa on the success of the show, the temperature had dropped several more degrees.

"Brr," Winter said, as Luca cranked up the heat in his vehicle.

"It's a cold night out there," he agreed, rubbing her hands to transfer some of his own warmth to her.

It was a typical Luca thing to do, to consider her comfort ahead of his own. But his innate kindness was only one of the reasons she'd fallen head over heels for this wonderful—if frustratingly oblivious—man.

"Any chance I can talk you into making hot cocoa when we get home?" she asked, not eager for the night to end.

"All you have to do is ask," he told her.

And maybe it was that simple when she wanted a warm drink, but when she wanted him to share her bed and tried to tell him so, he'd responded that the sofa wasn't so bad.

Was he really that obtuse?

Was she being too subtle?

Or was the problem something else entirely? Maybe he hadn't been unaware of what she was offering but was simply uninterested?

Don't mistake lack of action for lack of interest, cariño.

The echo of his words made her blood hum in her veins and renewed her determination to show him that she was just as interested as he was—and maybe, finally, prepared to take action.

When they got back to their cabin, Luca opted to start a fire first, and while he was busy with that, Winter swapped her dress for a bulky sweater, fleece leggings and wool socks.

As she watched the flames dance in the fireplace and listened to him move about the kitchen, she had no cause to complain about their life together. He was a good man, thoughtful and kind, a good husband, attentive and helpful, and she knew he'd be a wonderful father to their child.

And yet, the more time she spent with Luca, the more she found herself wanting…more.

She wanted a *real* marriage in which they didn't just chat about their respective days across the dinner table but shared quiet conversations as they drifted off to sleep at night in their shared bed. Something that wasn't ever going to happen so long as he stubbornly insisted on bunking down in the living room.

Sometimes she caught him looking at her in a way that gave her hope he might want her as much as she wanted him. Then he'd realize he'd been caught looking at her, and he'd look away or take a step back, leaving her to wonder if maybe she'd imagined the desire in his eyes.

Still, there was a definite crackle of electricity in the air whenever he stood close—a charged awareness that made her body tingle and yearn.

She'd felt that same crackle tonight, as he looked at her in the restaurant, when his thigh brushed against hers at the recital, when he held her hands in his truck. And it made her think—hope— that tonight they might take a step forward in their relationship.

She was mulling over the possibilities when he settled on the sofa beside her, offering her one of the two mugs he carried.

"Thanks." She wrapped both hands around the cup, welcoming the warmth against her palms. Her cheeks were warm now, too, though that was the result of her steamy imagination more than the steaming beverage.

As they sipped their drinks, they talked about the pageant— their favorite parts, the most surprising parts and the thundering ovation at the end. During a lull in the conversation, Winter glanced over at Luca and couldn't hold back the giggle that slipped between her lips.

"What's funny?" he asked.

"You've got marshmallow on your nose."

"Do I?" He crossed his eyes to see, then leaned forward and rubbed his nose against hers. "Now you do, too."

He was being playful, but the close contact—however brief— had the effect of charging the air between them.

Their eyes locked and held.

Luca drew back, but didn't break that connection.

Winter held her breath, waiting.

He set his mug aside and rubbed his nose with the back of his hand to remove any sticky remnants. Next he gently wiped the marshmallow from her nose, maintaining eye contact all the while.

Winter didn't protest when he removed the mug from her hands and set it next to his.

And she definitely didn't object when he kissed her—she was too busy kissing him back!

His lips tasted of marshmallow and chocolate and something else—something darker and richer—that she recognized now as Luca's unique flavor. Without breaking the kiss, he shifted closer. His hand slid up her back, his fingers sifting through her hair to cup the back of her head, changing the angle of their kiss. His tongue traced the seam of her lips and slipped between them when they parted.

Their first kiss had started as a cautious exploration that quickly became something more. The second had been a formality to seal the vows they'd made in front of family and friends. The third had started playful and turned passionate—and then was interrupted. This kiss wasn't like any of those kisses. This time, when his mouth came down on hers, it was hot and hungry, and she responded with a passion that equaled his.

But all too soon, Luca drew back.

"*Dios.* Winter... *Lo lamento tanto.* I'm so sorry."

She blinked. "Why are you apologizing?"

"I crossed the line."

"The only line is the one you've drawn," she told him.

"And I shouldn't have crossed it."

"I'm confused," she admitted. "If you're attracted to me and I'm attracted to you—and I am—why is there even a line between us?"

"Because I'm supposed to be helping you, not taking advantage of you."

She pushed to her feet, visibly frustrated. "*Me vuelves loco,*" she muttered. "You're not taking advantage of me, but you are making me crazy."

"You don't feel as though I'm taking advantage of you right now because you're grateful to me," he acknowledged ruefully.

"I *am* grateful to you," she confirmed. "I'm also wildly attracted to you, and if you stopped—*por un maldito minuto*—assuming you knew what was best for me and actually asked me what I wanted, I'd tell you that I want you to kiss me again."

He opened his mouth as if to reply, then closed it again without saying a word.

"*Hombre estúpido*," she muttered, her tone a combination of exasperation and affection, as she lowered herself to straddle his lap.

Then *she* kissed *him*, again and again, until they were both panting and breathless.

Though she wasn't entirely sure her legs would support her, Winter rose to her feet once more and reached for his hand.

"Come to bed with me, Luca," she urged.

"This will change things," he cautioned, even as he willingly followed her lead.

"*Gracias a Dios.*"

But as soon as the bedroom door closed, Winter suddenly seemed shy and uncertain.

"Second thoughts?" Luca asked gently.

She immediately shook her head, and he exhaled a silent, grateful sigh of relief.

"I want to make love with you," she said. "I just hope you aren't…disappointed."

"I'm not going to be disappointed, *cariño*."

"You don't know that."

"Yes, I do," he insisted. "Because the fact that it's actually going to happen—here, now, tonight—is everything I've been thinking about for the past two weeks. Night and day."

She offered him a small smile then, but he could tell she wasn't entirely convinced—and once again, he found himself wishing he could have just ten minutes alone with her ex-husband to make him regret the scars he'd left on this incredible woman.

"Can I make a suggestion?" Luca said to her now.

"Okay," she agreed.

"Stop worrying and enjoy the moment."

"I'm hoping it will take more than a moment."

He chuckled softly as he lifted her sweater over her head and tossed it aside. "Well, I've wanted you for so long, I'm not making any guarantees."

She unbuttoned his flannel shirt and pushed it over his shoulders.

Of course, it was December in Montana, so they'd both dressed in layers. Next she removed his thermal undershirt, exposing his wide chest, broad shoulders, bronzed skin and tight muscles. Then he dispensed with her long-sleeved T-shirt, beneath which she was wearing a simple white cotton bra, her full breasts barely contained by the cups.

Though he was eager to unfasten the clasp and fill his hands with her, he turned his attention to her leggings first, hooking his fingers in the waistband and pulling them over her hips and down her legs. Beneath the curve of her belly, her bikini panties were blue—and covered with smiling yellow daisies that made him smile. On her feet were thick wool socks.

His smile widened.

"I didn't plan on this when I got changed," she confided. "Or I might have put on sexier underwear."

"I don't think I could handle anything sexier," he told her. "Because you make smiling daisies unbelievably sexy."

His compliment warmed her all the way to her toes.

Still, she had to ask, "Even with a baby belly?"

"Even with a baby belly," he confirmed, gently caressing the swell of her tummy.

Then he kissed her again, and her mind went blank.

Somehow, between kisses, he managed to get rid of his jeans and socks and pull back the covers of the bed. As he eased her onto the mattress, he covered her body with his own.

She'd been dreaming about making love with Luca since their first kiss. She'd imagined how it might feel to have his hands on her body, and now they were there. His callused palms were moving over her bare flesh, and the reality was so much better than fantasy.

He made his way down her body, caressing and kissing every inch of her skin, and the onslaught of glorious sensations was almost too much to bear.

Winter's limited sexual experience had been gained at the rough hands of her husband. Matt had always focused on his own pleasure, unconcerned with that of his wife. He'd suck on her neck, branding her with his mouth, or pinch her nipples a little too hard, smiling when she winced. Only once had she dared ask him to stop when he was hurting her, and he'd immediately chastised her for being no fun and berated her for ruining his pleasure.

She shoved those memories aside, refusing to let them shadow her experience with Luca. She knew that he'd be careful with her—it wasn't in his nature to be anything else—and she trusted that the experience would be enjoyable. Of course, she knew better now than to expect the kind of earth-shattering climax she'd read about in the romance novels that had always been her escape from reality, but the way Luca made her feel when he kissed her and touched her gave her hope that she would finally learn what all the fuss was about.

Still, she was shocked to realize how incredibly aroused she was already. She could feel the dampness of her desire between her thighs, making her ready for him. Making her yearn for him with a desperation she'd never known before.

"We probably should have talked about condoms before now," Luca said, when he came up for air after kissing her again.

"I can't get more pregnant," she told him.

"There are reasons to take precautions other than birth control," he pointed out gently.

"Right," she realized, her cheeks flushing.

"I'm not in the habit of having unprotected sex," he told her. "And though I didn't dare let myself hope this would ever happen, I did see my doctor before we were married, so that I could assure you there was nothing to worry about."

She thought she'd be embarrassed to have this conversation, but she appreciated that Luca had brought up the topic beforehand rather than having cause for regrets afterward.

"I've only ever been with Matt," she said. "But I know he cheated on me and I don't know if he was careful. So I asked my doctor to test me, too, because I was worried not just about me but about my baby. Thankfully, all the tests came back clear."

"So after pausing things to ask the awkward questions, I don't have to pause again to rummage in my drawer for a condom?" he prompted.

"I appreciate you pausing to ask the awkward questions," she assured him. "And no condom required."

"Good to know," he said, then dipped his head to draw her nipple into his mouth.

She tensed, bracing herself for the pain of his teeth. But he only swirled his tongue around, laving the turgid peak. Unexpected pleasure pulsed in her veins, eliciting a low moan from deep in her throat. He responded by suckling her breast, the gentle tugs of his mouth causing corresponding tugs low in her belly.

Growing pleasure pushed aside any lingering vestiges of apprehension, and she felt herself relax into the mattress as Luca made his way down her body. He alternated lingering kisses with teasing licks and gentle nibbles, as if he was a starving man and she was a feast for him to sample and savor.

He nudged her thighs apart, and her muscles quivered as her legs fell open. His fingertips trailed from her ankles to her knees, higher. There was so much liquid heat inside her, she felt as if it was dripping out of her body, right where his thumbs parted the folds of skin at her center. He groaned, a sound of deep male satisfaction, when he discovered that she was wet and ready.

And she was ready for what came next, digging her heels into the mattress and bracing herself for his entry. He was huge and hard and she was the teensiest bit concerned about the logistics of fitting their bodies together, but that apprehension was no match for the desire that pulsed in her veins.

She gasped in shock when instead he lowered his head and put his mouth on her. Right there, where she could feel herself throbbing with need. And gasped again in response to the unexpected wave of pleasure that swamped her when his tongue dipped inside.

She knew that some men enjoyed pleasuring women this way, but Matt had not been one of them. Though he liked to see her on her knees, he refused to demean himself—his words—in the same way.

Thankfully that memory dissipated almost as soon as it materialized, so there was nothing but glorious sensation as Luca licked and sucked, making her feel things she'd never imagined she might feel.

Her breath was coming in fast, shallow pants, tension coiling deep in her belly as he continued to hold her open for his mouth, not just tasting but devouring her.

There was so much pleasure. Maybe too much pleasure. Winter didn't want him to stop, but she wasn't sure how much more she could stand before she simply…shattered.

Another whimper. A throaty moan.

Were those sounds coming from her?

She'd never been so vocal before.

Never felt what she was feeling right now.

"Let go," Luca urged.

She wasn't sure if she heard him speak the words or simply

felt them reverberate through her body. She needed to reply, to tell him that she couldn't. That she didn't know how.

But before she could form the words to respond, it happened.

A hoarse, shocked cry announced her surrender as she let go—and launched like a rocket hurtling into space, surrounded by so much heat and light and intensity, she shattered into a million pieces.

A million pieces suspended in the black of space for a long moment, shining bright against the darkness before fading away.

She didn't realize she was crying until she felt the brush of his fingertips on her cheeks, wiping the tears.

"You okay?" he asked gently.

She managed to nod. "I didn't know…"

The words trailed off, her cheeks burning with humiliation.

For God's sake, she'd been married! For four years, she'd been married and not even realized how innocent she was in so many ways.

"Now you do," he said, just the hint of a smile curving his lips. "And now that I know what that does to you, I'm going to want to do it again and again."

Her cheeks burned hotter.

"Your turn now," she said, shifting onto her knees on the bed so that she could reciprocate.

He caught her around the middle and flipped her gently onto her back again. "Let's save that for another time."

"But…don't you want…?"

He smiled, his gaze hot and intense. "I definitely want, but I wanted to give you a minute to catch your breath before the next part."

"I'm ready," she told him.

He wondered if she knew that she sounded more resigned than enthusiastic, and once again found himself wanting to throttle Matt Hathaway with his bare hands for failing to show this bright, beautiful, amazing woman that lovemaking was something to be shared and treasured rather than endured.

It was obvious to Luca that she'd been surprised by her own pleasure, and it made him determined to show her a whole lot more. He settled between her legs now, because she seemed eager to get on with it. But instead of driving into her wet heat, he nudged at the slick opening with the tip of his erection, teasing a little, testing her response. Then he lowered his head and kissed her, long and slow and deep, until he felt the tension ease from her body as she responded to his kiss.

"Luca." His name was a whispered plea on her lips.

"Tell me what you want," he urged. "What you need."

"You," she said. "Please, Luca. I need you inside me."

It was a plea he couldn't ignore and didn't want to deny, because he wanted the same thing.

Still, he took his time, easing into her slowly, giving her time to accept and adjust.

"Okay?" he asked, when he was finally buried to the hilt.

She nodded. "It's good. Really good."

It was there in her voice again—just a hint of surprise that made him want to surprise her more.

"It's going to get better," he promised.

"I don't know if I can handle better," she admitted.

"Let's find out."

He captured her mouth again as he began to move inside her.

Every time she thought she couldn't possibly take any more, feel any more, Luca proved her wrong. He grasped her feet to hook her ankles behind his back, a subtle shift that, impossible as it seemed, allowed him to sink even deeper inside her. The new position created greater friction where they were joined. Unbelievably glorious friction that worked with his long, deep strokes to push her toward the pinnacle of pleasure again.

This time, when she tumbled over, he went with her.

Chapter Twelve

It took several long minutes for Luca to catch his breath and several more after that before he could summon the energy to move. When he managed to lift his weight off Winter and collapse beside her, he saw that she was equally sated and spent. And as hot as she'd looked in the clingy red dress she'd worn to the concert earlier, he decided his absolute favorite outfit was what she was wearing right now—nothing but a satisfied smile on her lips.

He lifted a hand to brush an errant strand of hair away from her face. Her eyelids flickered and slowly opened.

He brushed his lips over hers gently. "Thank you for inviting me to your bed."

That sexy smile widened. "Thank you for finally accepting my invitation."

"And now that I have, I'm never sleeping on that sofa again," he told her.

"You might change your mind when I'm nine months pregnant and taking up more than half the mattress."

"Nope. Never," he promised, splaying his hand over her belly.

She laid her hand on top of his.

"It still surprises me sometimes to think that there's an actual little person growing inside you," he mused.

"According to my book, the baby's only about the size of a bell pepper right now," she told him. "So I'm not sure why my stomach has expanded to the size of a salad bowl."

He chuckled softly at that. "Because your uterus has to accommodate the placenta and amniotic fluid, too."

"You've been reading my book," she realized.

"You left it in the living room the other day. I was curious."

"I'm impressed."

"That I can read?"

She nudged him playfully with her elbow. "That you were interested enough to want to read it."

"It's fascinating, really, the changes that happen to a woman's body during pregnancy—and the way a woman's body is able to adapt to make room for her baby."

"Are you telling me that your apparent fascination with my body is about our baby?"

"No, it's about your incredible curves. Also—" he nuzzled her throat "—your incredibly addictive scent."

"My scent?"

"I can't figure out if it's your hair or your skin," he confided. "But it's been driving me crazy for weeks, haunting my dreams."

"I don't usually wear perfume," she said. "So maybe my body wash?"

"I have to hold my breath sometimes when I'm near you, because just breathing in that scent makes me hard."

"Really?" She sounded absurdly pleased by his confession.

"Really," he confirmed. "And though it's not easy—or comfortable—to walk around in a semiaroused state, you should expect to find a case of that body wash under the tree at Christmas."

"And what would you like to find under the tree at Christmas?" she asked.

He shrugged. "I can't think of anything I really want or need."

"That's not helpful," she chided.

"Christmas was never extravagant in our house," he told

her. "But my mom always made sure that we each got three gifts—one thing that we wanted, one that we needed and something to read."

"I like that," Winter said. "I think we should follow that guideline—and adopt the same philosophy for our child, to ensure he or she doesn't end up spoiled."

Luca appreciated how easily she said *our child* without even pausing to think about it, as if she believed the baby she carried was his baby, too. Certainly he'd started to feel proprietary about the child in her womb—and even more so after the ultrasound, when he'd gotten a first glimpse of the tiny person growing inside her.

But presumption of paternity notwithstanding, he knew he didn't have any real claim to her baby. What if she later changed her mind about wanting to be married to him?

Sure, everything was great between them now, but he couldn't help but worry that her feelings for him didn't go any deeper than the gratitude she'd confessed to feeling on their wedding night.

And as much as he hoped that she never had to see Matt Hathaway again, what would happen when she realized that her ex-husband was out of her life for good? When she could finally be certain that she and her baby were safe, would she still want to be with him?

He honestly didn't know—and that's why he had to be careful not to fall in love with her.

If it wasn't already too late…

"Do we have any plans for next weekend?" Luca asked, as they were tidying up the kitchen after dinner the following night.

"Other than the Santa Claus Parade, you mean?"

"I wasn't sure if you knew about that."

"There are signs up all over town," Winter pointed out. "I'd have to be pretty oblivious not to know about it."

"And you want to go?"

"I'm looking forward to it," she assured him.

"Temperatures are supposed to drop before then—it might be cold," he cautioned.

"I was born and raised in Montana. I know how to dress for the weather."

Which was the perfect segue for him to ask, "How do you feel about dressing like Mrs. Claus?"

"Mrs. Claus?" It didn't take long for the confusion in her eyes to give way to understanding—and perhaps a hint of amusement. "Are you telling me that you're Santa?"

"Well, not the real Santa Claus, obviously," he said.

"Obviously," she agreed.

"But my great-uncle and his new wife are the grand marshals of the parade this year and somehow—I'm still not sure how—I ended up being cast in the role of the jolly old man himself."

"Stanley and Winona, right?"

He nodded.

"I remember meeting them at the wedding. And I crossed paths with them again at the Silver Spur a couple weeks back."

"They're certainly memorable," he agreed.

"They were also big news when they were reunited earlier this year, after Winona went missing on what was supposed to be their wedding day."

"It was big news here," he acknowledged. "I didn't realize the story had made its way to Butte."

"I'm sure it made its way around the whole state," she said. "Everyone loves a happy ending—and Stanley and Winona definitely earned theirs."

"They did," he agreed. "But getting back to the parade…"

"What is Mrs. Claus expected to do?" Winter asked.

"Just sit next to Santa and smile and wave to everyone along the parade route."

"I think I can manage that."

"There's usually a small Christmas market set up in the square outside Town Hall the day of the parade, too," he told her. "With food booths and local artisans selling their wares. It's a good place to find handmade gift items, if you still need to do any shopping."

"Sounds like fun," she agreed.

"And then, when it gets dark, there's the ceremonial Christmas tree lighting. Everyone gathers in the town square to *ooh* and *ahh* when the mayor plugs in the lights."

"I never realized that Tenacity celebrated the holiday in such a big way."

"The residents do like to find reasons to come together as a community."

"It's one of the things I've learned to appreciate since I came back," Winter said. "Even if, as a kid, it seemed as if there was never anything to do here."

"You'd just graduated high school when you moved away," he pointed out. "Teenagers aren't exactly the target demographic of Santa Claus parades and Christmas tree lightings."

"True enough," she acknowledged. "And do we have any plans for after the Christmas tree lighting?"

He shook his head. "The rest of our night is free. Why—did you have something specific in mind?"

"I had several thoughts," she said, and leaned close to whisper them in his ear.

"That's quite the list," he noted. "I'm not sure we could manage all of that on Saturday."

"Then maybe we could check one or two off the list tonight?"

"Exactly what I was thinking," he said, and lifted her into his arms to carry her to the bedroom.

***

"Someone has an extra glow today," Sera remarked, when she settled into the seat across from Winter at the Silver Spur Café for what they'd decided would be their weekly coffee klatch.

Winter felt her cheeks grow warm. "It's possible I have a newfound appreciation for married life."

"So *Operation: Seduction* was a success."

"*Operation: Seduction* never got off the ground, because I didn't have the first clue where to begin," Winter confided. "But after the holiday concert the other night, Luca kissed me—and then apologized for kissing me. And then I got mad at him for apologizing and, well, one thing led to another. And another. And another." Her lips curved as she wrapped her hands around her cup. "And every night since then."

"Well." Sera waved her hand in front of her face. "Your groom might have been a little slow out of the gate, but apparently he's making up lost ground."

"I didn't expect to be this happy. I didn't know that I could be."

"You finally found the right someone for you," her friend said. "And I'm glad, because you deserve no less."

Winter appreciated her kind words, but she also realized that they'd spent far too much time talking about what was going on in her life, so she shifted the conversation to ask about the kids. And Sera told her about Nicolas's indecipherable letter to Santa, which had his parents worried about potential disappointment Christmas morning; Gabriel's role as a mooing sheep in the preschool nativity play—he was supposed to be a sheep because they only had sheep costumes, but he was adamant that he wanted to be a cow and agreed to wear the sheep costume only if he could moo like a cow; and Elena's stubborn refusal to let any kind of green vegetable cross her lips.

When they finally parted ways—Winter to go back to her

job at Castillo's and Sera to do her weekly grocery shopping before returning home to relieve Rafael of childcare duties—Winter realized that her deeper friendship with her cousin's wife was one more blessing to count in a life that was suddenly filled with so many.

"A delivery came while you were out," Roberto said, when she returned to the restaurant.

Winter pivoted away from the door that led to the office and made her way to the bar.

She caught the scent before she saw the flowers.

Roses.

She knew that most roses sold in florist shops had little or no scent, having been bred for appearance and durability rather than their smell. But she had such strong and negative memories linked to the flowers that just a hint of the scent was enough to make her stomach churn. As it was churning now.

Because that hint of a scent was multiplied by dozens.

Dozens and dozens.

They weren't from Luca—he would never send her roses.

Only one person had ever done so.

"Throw them out," she told Roberto.

He gaped at her. "You can't be serious. There's about ten dozen flowers here."

She battled against the nausea that churned in her stomach. "I don't want them."

"I can't just toss them," he protested.

"Then do whatever you want with them," she said, not wanting her boss's son to know how badly she was shaking inside. "But please get them out of here."

"Okay." He nodded. "Do you want the card at least?"

She started to shake her head, then reconsidered.

She didn't want the card—she didn't need to read the message to know the flowers were from Matt and that this was just his latest move in what was obviously another one of his twisted mind games—but since she'd already filed a report with the police, she might as well include an addendum.

"Okay," she finally said. "I'll take the card."

When Roberto handed it to her, her gaze automatically shifted to the text.

A rose for every day that we've been apart—and every day that you've been on my mind.

Luca could tell that Winter had been shaken by the flower delivery, though she pretended she wasn't. And he was frustrated that the police seemed unwilling to do anything, though he understood that it wasn't against the law to send flowers—not even to an ex-wife. It was little consolation to him that Matt had sent the wedding photo to Winter at her cousin's address and the flowers to her work, suggesting that while he apparently knew she was in Tenacity, he didn't have any more specific information than that.

But to keep Winter from worrying too much about what her ex-husband might do next, Luca tried to keep her busy with seasonal activities and preparations for the holiday, which she embraced wholeheartedly. And today, finally, was the Santa Claus Parade.

A couple of teenagers dressed as Santa's elves carried the hand-lettered banner announcing, "Tenacity's Annual Santa Claus Parade." The grand marshals followed immediately behind in a horse-drawn carriage that jingled with bells. (Horses borrowed from Julian Sanchez's The Start of a New Day Ranch and carriage on loan from Edward Dalton.) Stanley Sanchez looked happy and dapper in his sheepskin-lined leather jacket and cowboy hat; Winona sat beside him, beaming, in her puffy red coat and Santa hat, with her favorite purple cowboy boots on her feet.

Following behind the grand marshals were a number of floats representing various community groups, including the Tenacity Quilting Club—the members of whom were actually stitching squares as they rode down the street, the Tenacity Fund for Dinosaurs—with Andrea Spence and Seth Taylor and inflatable dinosaurs wearing Santa hats and holding brightly wrapped gifts, the Tenacity Foundation—with Barrett Deroy and Brent Woodson and an assortment of props from the town's glory days doing double duty as Christmas tree decorations, and the Multicultural Society depicting holidays around the world.

Interspersed between the various floats were other local groups that marched along the route—such as the high school band and cheer squad, the local Cub Scouts, members of a youth karate club, grade school minor hockey players wearing their jerseys and carrying their sticks and a contingent of lumberjacks—with bushy beards and plaid shirts and prop axes in hand—from Hendrick's Farm.

Of course, the main attraction of the Santa Claus Parade was always Santa, so the decorated platform that carried Santa's sleigh and his reindeer came at the very end, which meant that Luca and Winter were sitting for a very long time waiting to join the procession.

Just as they started moving, Winter tipped her head back against his shoulder, smiling up at the sky. "Look, Luca—it's snowing."

"So it is," he noted.

"Now it really feels like Christmas," she said happily.

"We're still five days out from the twenty-fifth," he felt compelled to remind her.

"I'd accuse you of raining on my parade, but Mother Nature obviously has a better plan for today."

He chuckled at that. "She certainly set the scene for the festivities."

A gust of wind swooped down then, making the snowflakes swirl and Winter shiver.

He pulled a blanket over her lap. "Does that help?"

She nodded. "A little."

He snuggled closer.

"Much better," she said.

As Santa's sleigh made its way along the parade route, Winter almost forgot about her frozen fingers and toes, amazed as she was to see the street was crowded with people young and old, the residents of Tenacity having come out in full force to celebrate the season. And despite the cold temperature, everyone was in good spirits—especially the little ones, who cheered excitedly when Santa waved and ho-ho-hoed in their direction.

"I don't know about you, but I'm starving," Luca said, when they exited the sleigh at the end of the parade route.

"Breakfast was a long time ago," Winter agreed.

"We should be able to find something at the food booths."

"But first we need to get out of these costumes. If you show up in the town square dressed like that, you'll be mobbed by kids," she cautioned.

"Fair point," he acknowledged.

Not that she didn't think he could handle it. Over the past few weeks, she'd learned that her husband had an easy way with little ones as she'd enjoyed watching him with Emery and Jay and Robbie. Those interactions further solidified her conviction that he was going to be a great dad. The kind of dad her baby deserved. A dad that he or she could look up to, who treated his wife with consideration and respect and would provide an example of a healthy, supportive relationship.

"You were a wonderful Santa," she told him now. "And enthusiastic enough to convince the kids that you're the real deal."

"As if the real Santa could take time away from his duties this close to Christmas to ride in a small town parade," Luca scoffed.

"If Santa's magic allows him to deliver presents across the globe in one night, surely it can allow him to participate in community events and enjoy visits to shopping malls."

"Maybe it could," he allowed. "But he doesn't have to do

those things because he has an army of minions to perform those menial tasks."

"Is that what your parents told you when you were a kid? That Santa had an army of minions?" she asked, amused.

"Actually, they said it was a group of volunteer helpers."

"That's pretty creative," she noted.

"How did your parents explain the presence of a Santa on every corner to you?"

"They said that if I was old enough to question the sightings of so many fat men in red suits, I was old enough to know that Santa was just a myth."

"How old were you?" he wondered.

"Five."

Luca frowned at that. "I don't know how old I was when I found out the truth," he confided. "Probably eight or nine. But I had to pretend to believe for several more years, to maintain the illusion for Nina and Marisa."

"You're a good brother."

"I'm happy to let you believe that," he said. "But it's probably more accurate to say that I was afraid of my mother's wrath. Not that she ever hit us," he hastened to assure her. "Or even raised her voice, really. She didn't have to, because we knew there were consequences for unacceptable behavior—usually losing some kind of privilege or having to do extra chores."

"I'll bet you did a lot of extra chores."

"Not as many as Diego," he assured her.

"Well, I've got a chore for you now."

"What's that?"

"Help me out of this dress so we can take it, along with your suit, back to the warehouse."

"Undressing you isn't a chore, it's a pleasure," he assured her. "In fact, I think that after we get rid of these clothes, we should go home and get rid of the rest of our clothes."

"As tempting as that is—" and it was admittedly very tempting "—you promised we could stay for the tree lighting."

"We have a tree at home. It's got lights."

"You also said you wanted to eat," Winter reminded him.

"We've got food at home, too."

She laughed then, her heart filled with light and joy, and drew his mouth down to hers for a long, lingering kiss.

"I'll bet you're sorry now that you resisted me for so long, aren't you?" she murmured against his lips.

"I honestly don't know what I was thinking," he said.

"Right now, I'm thinking we should get out of here."

Chapter Thirteen

But when they got to the warehouse, they discovered that the volunteers responsible for putting away the props—including Santa's reindeer—had just dumped them on the floor instead of returning them to the designated shelves. And Luca and Winter couldn't, in good conscience, leave them abandoned there. So after they hung up their costumes—on the rack labeled "holiday wardrobe"—they set about putting the reindeer back in their assigned space.

"You shouldn't be bending and lifting," Luca protested, when Winter ignored his suggestion that she let him handle the task.

"I have a baby in my belly, not a hernia."

"Still," he said.

"The doctor said that moderate exercise during pregnancy is not only permitted but recommended."

"I'm sure she meant a leisurely walk around town, not lifting Rudolph over your head."

Winter looked at the reindeer in her hands. "This can't be Rudolph. His nose isn't red."

"Okay, not lifting Dasher or Dancer or Prancer or Vixen or—"

"Also," she said, interrupting his recital of reindeer names, "it's made of paper-mache and probably doesn't weigh as much as a ten-pound bag of potatoes."

"Which you shouldn't be lifting, either."

She huffed out a breath as she slid the reindeer onto the

shelf. "I appreciate your concern. Really. But I'm not incompetent or incapable."

"No, you're not."

His immediate agreement took some of the wind from her sails.

"You're a smart, strong, amazing woman who's growing a smart, strong, amazing baby."

And there went the last of the wind.

"Sometimes you manage to say exactly the right thing," she said, her tone begrudging.

"And sometimes I say completely the wrong thing," he acknowledged.

"That's true," she agreed, reaching for another reindeer. "I'm trying not to hold that against you."

"If I told you that you have an incredibly sexy body, would you hold that against me?" he asked hopefully.

"Anytime, anywhere," she promised.

He smiled and dipped his head to brush his lips against hers. Then he took the last reindeer from her hands and lifted it onto the shelf above her head. But it didn't slide into place as easily as its companions, and its antlers were hanging precariously over the edge.

So Luca gave it another push. Apparently he shoved a little too hard, so that the reindeer bumped against whatever was on the shelf behind it—and bumped it right off the other side.

"Fu—dge," he said.

"I didn't hear a crash, so I don't think you broke anything," Winter noted, making her way around to the back of the shelving unit.

"Nope. Nothing broken," she confirmed. "Just dented the box."

But as she bent to gather up the contents that had spilled out, her breath caught, then expelled in a whoosh. "Oh."

Curious to know what had captured her attention, Luca followed her path and found her kneeling on the floor, folded papers scattered in front of her.

Not papers, he realized.

Ballots.

He snagged one for a closer look. "Look at the names. These ballots are from last month's mayoral election," he said.

"Do you notice anything else?" Winter asked.

He crouched beside her to examine a few more.

"Almost all of them have Xs in the box beside JenniLynn Garrett's name," she pointed out.

"What are they doing here?" he wondered aloud.

"I don't know, but I know there are rules and procedures regarding the handling of election materials. And I'm pretty sure they're supposed to be stored in sealed containers in a secure location—not shoved in a banker's box in a random warehouse."

"What are you doing?" he asked, when she pulled out her phone and began snapping photos.

"Documenting the evidence."

"Evidence of what?"

"Possible election tampering," she said.

"It's also possible the ballots are only evidence of careless storage," he felt compelled to point out to her.

"Do you really think so?" she asked dubiously.

"I don't know what to think."

"Well, I have a bad feeling about this," she confided. "I think we should call the police."

"Maybe we should talk to Marty Moore before we involve the authorities," he suggested. "Considering we don't have any proof that a crime was committed."

"You want to talk to the mayor? Who won the election by only a handful of votes—and definitely a lot fewer than the number in this box in favor of JenniLynn Garrett?"

"You're assuming all the ballots are the same as these ones," he said, indicating those in his hand.

"Let's find out," she said.

"If those ballots are evidence of a crime, as you suggested, you might be accused of tampering with evidence—and I don't want our baby born behind bars."

She looked at him then, a radiant smile on her face. "You just said *our baby*."

"I did," he confirmed. "But the part of my statement that I wanted you to focus on was the *behind bars* part."

"No one's going to put me in jail," she assured him, already sorting the ballots according to vote.

"I'd really rather not test that theory."

"But if I *was* put in jail, would you come visit me?"

He sighed. "As if I'd be able to stay away."

She glanced up to smile at him again, then returned to her counting.

"Thirty-nine votes for JenniLynn Garrett, fourteen for Ellis Corey and six for Graham Callahan," she announced, her expression troubled now. "These votes would have changed the results of the election."

"Assuming they weren't counted."

She returned the ballots and set the lid back on top of the box. "Which seems more reasonable than assuming they were counted then randomly tossed in a box and hidden in a warehouse."

He couldn't argue with that.

"Okay," he said, relenting. "I'll call Marty."

"You're really going to call the man who barely won the election to tell him that we found ballots that might change the outcome?"

"If he was somehow involved in any tampering, I think we should give him a chance to do the right thing."

"What makes you think someone who'd fix an election would want to do the right thing?"

"A perhaps foolish belief in the inherent goodness of mankind."

"Go ahead, then," she said.

Of course, he first had to look up the directory of town council members to find his contact information. And then his call went unanswered.

Winter glanced at her watch. "It's almost time for the tree lighting. If we head back to the town square, we should be able to catch him there."

So they made their way back to the center of the festivities, grabbed a couple of burgers from one of the food booths, then tracked down the mayor by the stage, chatting with a member of his staff. They finished their burgers, then waited for him to finish his conversation before stepping forward.

"Mr. Moore," Luca said.

Marty turned around. "Can I help you?"

"I'm Luca Sanchez," he said, introducing himself. "And this is my wife, Winter."

"Santa and Mrs. Claus," the mayor said, nodding an acknowledgment. "What can I do for you?"

"After the parade, we went to return our costumes to the warehouse behind the community center—"

"I didn't think that warehouse was used anymore," Marty remarked, giving them his full attention now.

"Primarily for storing seasonal decorations, or so it seemed," Luca said.

"I wasn't aware of that," Marty admitted.

"If the warehouse isn't in use, doesn't it seem odd to you that there would be a box of ballots from the recent election inside?" Winter asked him.

The mayor's Adam's apple bobbed as he swallowed. "The local elections administrator is supposed to shred any unused ballots," he said. "But there was a new administrator this year. Perhaps he misunderstood that requirement and put them into storage instead."

"Would the elections administrator have access to that storage space?"

"Tenacity isn't exactly Fort Knox," the mayor noted dryly.

"I suspect anyone who asked one of the town clerks for access would be given the code to the lock with few questions asked—just as you were."

He was quick on his feet, Winter noted, with a ready answer to every question. But he also had a bead of sweat rolling slowly from his brow down the side of his face.

"You're sure the ballots in the warehouse were unused?" Winter pressed.

"Positive," Marty assured her. "All of the assigned ballots were counted and then secured in official election boxes."

Apparently that was his story and he was sticking to it.

"If there's nothing else, I've got official duties to attend to," he said, dismissing them along with their concerns.

"Of course," Luca agreed. "Apologies for wasting your time."

"It's always a pleasure to chat with constituents," Marty replied, not sounding pleased at all.

"You didn't believe a word he said, did you?" Winter asked, as Luca steered her away from the stage.

"Only the part about Tenacity not being Fort Knox," he told her. "But that still doesn't prove election tampering."

"Why don't you want to believe he could have fixed the election?"

"I just can't imagine that *anyone* would want to be mayor of this town badly enough to cheat."

"Tenacity might not be Billings or Missoula, but the mayor wields a fair amount of power in this town, and I think that Marty Moore got a taste of that power as acting mayor and didn't want to let go of it."

"He certainly didn't like being asked questions, did he?" Luca mused.

"Are we going to call the police now?" Winter prompted.

"No need," he said. "Almost everyone in town is here, so we shouldn't have to look too hard to find a member of local law enforcement."

She smiled. "But after the tree lighting, right? Since it's almost that time, anyway."

"After the tree lighting," he agreed.

Of course, before the main event, the mayor took advantage of his captive audience to give a speech extolling the wonders of the town and expressing his gratitude to the people who'd entrusted him to guide Tenacity into a newer and brighter future.

"Is it possible to have an older future?" Winter wondered aloud.

"It's possible to have a duller one," an elderly gentleman with obviously sharp hearing responded. "Which Marty Moore will undoubtedly deliver."

"If we were sincerely concerned about global warming, we'd put time limits on his speeches," another man chimed in. "All Marty does is blow hot air."

"And yet, he somehow got elected," Winter remarked.

"Somehow indeed," a woman agreed with obvious pique.

Finally Marty wrapped up his speech, concluding with a shout of "Merry Christmas" before he *finally* threw the switch to illuminate the twenty-foot tree with hundreds—maybe thousands—of lights.

There was a collective gasp from the crowd, followed by cheers and applause.

And then, whether spontaneous or rehearsed, someone in the crowd—Marisa, was Winter's guess—sang out the opening lines of "O Christmas Tree." Soon a few other voices joined in, then a few more, and by the end of the first verse, it sounded as if the whole crowd was singing. It was an anthem to the holiday that held everyone spellbound until the final lyrics were carried away on the breeze.

When the gathering finally dispersed, Winter and Luca set off on their quest.

"Over there," she said, pointing to where a couple of uniformed police officers were warming their hands around paper cups of steaming coffee.

The officers—Perry and Karlsson—didn't seem particularly interested as Luca and Winter explained what they'd found in the warehouse, but in the end, they agreed that someone should check it out—and they proceeded to engage in a game of rock-paper-scissors to decide who that someone would be.

Karlsson threw paper and was beaten by Perry's scissors.

"Only rookies throw paper," Luca said, as the officer led them to his cruiser.

"I know," Karlsson admitted. "But Perry's got plans with his girl later tonight and, in the off chance that this turns out to be something, I didn't want him to have to stand her up."

"You're a good friend," Winter noted.

"Or maybe still feeling the sting of being dumped by my girl for missing out on too many Saturday nights."

Despite his conversational demeanor, Winter could tell that the officer didn't expect to find anything at the warehouse. But she didn't mind that he was skeptical, because she knew the evidence would prove them right.

As it turned out, though, they didn't even have a chance to go inside. When Officer Karlsson turned into the drive leading to the warehouse, his vehicle headlights illuminated Marty Moore putting something in the trunk of his vehicle.

"That looks like the box we found," Luca told Karlsson.

"The one with the ballots he claimed were unused," Winter added.

"So why would he be interested in a box of unused ballots?" the officer mused.

"Let's find out," Luca suggested.

Karlsson pulled up beside Marty's car, then stepped out of his vehicle and opened the back door so that Luca and Winter could exit.

"Good evening, Mr. Mayor," the officer said.

Marty quickly closed his trunk before turning to respond. "Good evening, Officer."

Karlsson tucked his hands in his pockets and rocked back on his heels, assuming a deliberately casual posture. "Thought you might have hung around the town square for a while after the tree lighting, chatting with your constituents."

"I'm always available to do so," the mayor responded. "But I prefer to chat in the warmth of my office rather than standing in the snow."

"Fair enough," Karlsson noted. "So what brings you out here tonight?"

"Just taking care of some unfinished business."

"Business, huh? At—" the officer drew a hand out of his pocket to check his watch "—nine o'clock on a Saturday night?"

"The work of a public servant is never done," Marty pointed out. "Though I don't suppose I have to tell you that."

"No, sir," Karlsson agreed. "And hopefully you understand that I'm doing my job as a public servant when I ask you to open your trunk for me, please."

"Open my trunk?" Marty echoed. "Why?"

"Because I saw you put a box in there."

"I'm not aware of any law that prohibits a man from operating a motor vehicle with a box in his trunk."

"It's more the contents of the box that I'm interested in," the officer told him.

"You haven't been with the police department very long, have you, Officer Karlsson?"

"No, sir," he confirmed.

"So perhaps you're unaware that your boss is a good friend of mine who won't be happy to hear that I was harassed by one of his junior officers."

"I don't know the chief's friends," Karlsson acknowledged. "But I know the chief. He's a tough but fair man who taught me everything I know about law enforcement and who would be happy to hear that I was doing my job."

"I'll be sure to share your glowing words when I have breakfast with him tomorrow," Marty said.

"You do that," the officer told him. "But right now, I need you to open your trunk."

"I have an expectation of privacy in my personal vehicle," the mayor argued. "And you don't have a warrant, so any search would be a violation of my Fourth Amendment rights."

"I don't need a warrant. I've got—" the officer paused, searching for the right word, before concluding "—extagent circumstances."

"I think you mean *exigent*," Marty said condescendingly.

Karlsson's face flushed. "Whatever the word is, I've got reasonable grounds to believe that there's evidence in your trunk that might be destroyed if not taken into my custody right now."

"Evidence of what?" the mayor challenged.

"Uncounted ballots from the last election," Winter said.

"I told you—the box you found contained unused ballots."

"That's what you said," she agreed. "But we saw the ballots—marked with Xs. Most of them cast for JenniLynn Garrett."

"You're mistaken," Marty snapped. "Or delusional."

"We both saw them," Luca chimed in.

"Open your trunk," Karlsson said again, this time in a tone that brooked no argument.

"They're unused ballots," Marty insisted, even as he finally relented to the request. "And I was simply going to dispose of them, as they should have been disposed of after the election."

The officer removed the lid from the box and peered inside.

"Ballots," he confirmed. He lifted out a handful and looked through them. "Unused ballots."

"No!" Winter said, stunned.

Marty smirked. "Can I go now?"

The officer dug deeper into the box. "And more that appear to have been marked by voters."

"Spoiled ballots," Marty said quickly.

"What's the criteria for determining if a ballot's spoiled?" Officer Karlsson asked.

"There are several things that can contribute to such a designation," Marty hedged.

"Such as voting for someone other than you?" Winter guessed.

Marty responded by glowering at her.

Luca and Winter waited until they saw Officer Karlsson put Marty in the back of his car, then they made their way back to the town square where Luca had parked his truck a lot of hours earlier.

"It's been an eventful day," he noted.

"And a long one," she said.

"You tired?"

"Actually, not as much as I thought I'd be. Or maybe my adrenaline is pumping because we got to be involved in the takedown of a criminal."

He chuckled. "I might think you've been watching too many crime shows on TV, except that the only thing I've ever seen you watch are Christmas movies."

"There are still several on my list that we haven't seen because we've found other ways to pass the time in recent evenings."

"Are you saying that you want to watch a Christmas movie tonight?" Luca asked.

Winter shook her head, a seductive smile playing at the corners of her mouth. "I'm saying I want to *not* watch a Christmas movie tonight."

And that's what they did.

Chapter Fourteen

"I wonder if Marty made it to his breakfast meeting with the police chief this morning," Luca mused, as he nibbled on a cinnamon roll.

"I hope he had to eat his eggs behind bars," Winter said, popping a last bite of bacon into her mouth.

"As satisfying as it might be to think that, you need to consider that he might already be out of jail."

"I know." She sipped her herbal tea. "I just like to believe we live in a world where people are held accountable for their actions."

He could tell by the heaviness of her tone that Winter wasn't thinking about Marty Moore but Matt Hathaway now.

"Regretting your decision not to press charges?" he asked cautiously.

Her hand automatically moved to the curve of her belly, an instinctive gesture he wasn't sure she was even aware of making when she was thinking about protecting her baby, but she shook her head.

"No. Even if I'd gone to the police, it's not likely they would have done anything, because I hadn't documented any of his abuse. I hadn't noted dates or details or taken pictures of the bruises he left on me, so my allegations would have been canceled out by his denials."

"Thankfully you were brave enough to leave," Luca pointed out.

"Was it brave?" she wondered aloud.

"Incredibly brave," he said.

"The whole time I was packing, I was shaking, terrified that his plans might change and he'd walk through the door again before I could get away."

"Isn't that the true definition of bravery—doing what needs to be done even when you're afraid?"

"You're asking me?" She pushed away from the table to carry her plate and cutlery to the sink.

"No." He shook his head. "I'm reminding you that you're brave and strong and amazing."

"I do feel braver—or at least stronger—now," she confided. "And I'm really glad you convinced me to stay in Tenacity."

"All it took was a marriage proposal and a shotgun wedding," he teased, adding his dishes to hers.

"And then twelve days to finally consummate our marriage."

"I assure you, I wouldn't have waited so long if I'd known how impatient you were."

She lifted her arms and looped them behind his head. "I honestly never imagined that I could be this happy. Every day that I wake up in your arms, I take a moment to count my blessings—and another moment to pray that Matt is out of my life forever."

"Your mom still keeps in touch with him, doesn't she?"

"I think it's more that he keeps in touch with her, and since I've made it clear to her that I don't want to talk about him, I don't feel like I can ask her if he's asked about me."

"Surely she'd give you a heads-up, though, if he did."

"I'd hope so. But Matt can be subtle and manipulative, and she might not even realize she's giving him information I don't want to share.

"On a more positive note, my friend Alice told me that he tried to get her to give up my address in Sacramento, since I asked her to let it slip that was where I was headed, and she thinks he made a trip to the west coast—because he apparently came back with a California girl. So I'm trying to be cautiously optimistic that he's accepted the divorce and moved on."

"I hope you're right. I don't like that you're living under a cloud of uncertainty."

"But I'm not letting that cloud cast any shadows on my life with you—not anymore," she promised.

"Still, it would be good for you to know that he's no longer a threat to you or your baby."

"*Our* baby," she reminded him.

He nodded, but he couldn't help wondering what it might mean for their future together if Winter's ex-husband had moved on. Their marriage was built on the foundation of her desire to provide a safe and stable home for the tiny life she carried inside her. And while he wanted to believe that their newfound closeness strengthened that foundation, he knew that she'd only accepted his proposal because she'd felt backed into a corner.

And when she was no longer in that corner, would she want to stay married to him?

"Earth to Luca."

He shook off the depressing thoughts and shifted his attention to his wife. "I'm here."

"But where'd you go?"

He decided he'd wasted enough time hiding his true feelings during their brief marriage and that he should be honest with her now. "I was just wondering—"

Before he could finish the thought, there was a knock on the door.

Winter glanced from him to the clock on the wall, a slight furrow marring her brow. "Who would be stopping by at nine o'clock on a Sunday morning?"

"That's a good question," he said, wondering if their brief conversation about his wife's ex-husband might somehow have conjured up his presence.

But even if Matt had followed Winter to Tenacity, it wasn't

likely that he would have tracked her to their cabin, more than a little off the beaten path.

To preempt further speculation, Luca crossed to the window and pulled back the curtain, revealing a vehicle with the local law enforcement logo on the door parked in the drive.

Not sure if he was relieved or alarmed to discover the police at his home, he opened the door to find Clayton Everett—the chief of police—standing there.

"Good morning, Mr. Sanchez."

"Is there a problem, Chief Everett?"

"Not at all," the lawman assured him. "I just stopped by to give you and your wife an update before the news was all over the media."

"News?" Luca prompted.

"Come in, Chief," Winter invited. "It's freezing outside and I just brewed a fresh pot of coffee."

"It's hard to say no to a hot drink on a cold day," the chief remarked as he stepped inside. "Thank you, ma'am."

"Cream and sugar?" she asked, leading the way to the kitchen.

"Just sugar, please. Two spoonfuls, if you don't mind."

Winter took a mug from the cupboard, added the requisite amount of sugar and filled it with fresh coffee from the carafe.

"Thank you, ma'am," he said again, accepting the proffered mug.

"Please, have a seat." She gestured to the small table where she and Luca had recently enjoyed their morning meal.

He accepted her invitation while she refilled Luca's mug and handed it to him.

"Thanks." He remained standing.

"I've interrupted your breakfast," the chief noted.

"We were finished," Winter assured him.

"So these cinnamon rolls here…?"

Unable to mistake the hopeful tone in his voice for anything else, she retrieved a plate from the cupboard. "Help yourself."

"Thank you, I think I will," he said, selecting a pastry.

"You said something about news?" Luca prompted, when Everett seemed content to nibble his roll and sip his coffee.

"Right." The chief wiped icing off his thumb with a paper napkin. "Well, the biggest headline will undoubtedly be the arrest of Marty Moore for election fraud—though, of course, you already know about that."

"So the ballots we found were deliberately set aside so they wouldn't be counted," Winter concluded.

Everett nodded. "Apparently Marty's campaign conducted some private polls before the election, which led him to believe that JenniLynn would come out on top. So he went to see her husband, because Rob Garrett had made no secret of the fact that he didn't want his wife to take on a job that would occupy too much of her time and cause her to neglect him."

"He does know this is the twenty-first century, doesn't he?" Luca asked.

"He claims to be a proponent of old-fashioned values," the chief explained. "Though he wasn't pleased when I questioned if stealing ballots was such a value."

Winter frowned. "Are you saying it was JenniLynn's husband who took the ballots?"

"That's what Marty claims. Of course, Rob denied it. But further investigation uncovered text messages between the two men that confirmed Marty's version of events and also provides evidence of conspiracy. Anyway, when the missing ballots were returned and all of the votes were recounted, JenniLynn Garrett came out the winner."

"So what happens to Marty Moore and Rob Garrett now?" Luca asked.

"They're both currently in lockup while the DA figures out who to charge with what," Everett said. "If either or both of them end up going to trial, it's possible the two of you will be called as witnesses, but I suspect, in light of the evidence, they'll opt to plead out their charges.

"Either way, this has created a scandal for the town, so the council plans to move quickly to swear in the new mayor and let JenniLynn set about righting the ship." The chief's mustache twitched then, as if he was fighting a smile. "According to my wife, women are always expected to clean up messes made by men—and it certainly seems to be true in this case."

He lifted his mug again to swallow the last mouthful of coffee, then pushed his chair back. "Thanks for the coffee break."

"Thank *you* for coming out here to give us the news," Winter said.

"Seemed like the right thing to do, seeing as how it was the two of you who found the evidence." He shook hands with each of them in turn, then made his way to the door.

"I can't believe JenniLynn's husband would steal ballots to sway the outcome of the election to keep his wife at home," Luca said, when the police chief had gone.

"I can," Winter said. "Because I was married to a man a little too much like Rob Garrett. Almost as soon as we were married, he started grumbling about my job taking too much of my time. And he didn't stop there. He started berating me for flirting with the guys at work—even though I'd never flirted with anyone before or after Matt.

"When I put on makeup to go to work, he demanded to know who I was trying to impress. If I wore a skirt, who was I showing my legs off to? If I went out for lunch, who was I meeting for a midday tryst?

"At first, I was confused. I didn't understand why he was saying those things and acting so irrationally. Had I done something to make him distrust me?"

"I can't imagine how difficult it must have been to live like that," Luca acknowledged.

"Even before our first anniversary, I wanted out of our marriage. Obviously I'd made a mistake, not only in agreeing to be his wife but also in believing myself in love with him. By then I'd realized the truth—that I'd only been infatuated. Duped and deceived by the man he pretended to be. I couldn't really love him because I'd never really known him. I'd only seen what he wanted me to see, just like everyone else." Her eyes closed, as if she didn't want to witness the past marching across her mind.

"Anyway—" she opened her eyes again to look at him and forced a smile "—I'm not going to waste any more time talking or even thinking about my ex-husband today."

"You've got better plans?" he asked, happy to follow her lead.

"I do," she confirmed, and this time her smile came easily. "Ice skating."

The next couple of days passed quickly and then, suddenly, it was the day before Christmas Eve and Luca and Winter were finalizing their holiday plans.

"It's tradition to have a big meal at my parents' house before church, but we can skip that, if you want," he said to his bride.

"What are you suggesting we skip—the meal or the service?"

He shrugged. "Whatever you want."

"I don't want to skip anything," she told him. "I don't want to miss a minute of the festivities with your family."

"Twenty-four hours from now, I'm going to remind you that you said that," he warned.

She laughed, but her expression quickly turned serious.

"You're thinking about your family?" he guessed.

She nodded. "They only moved to Texas six months ago, so this will be the first time I won't get to see them on Christmas Day."

"We probably could have made a trip to Dallas," he realized. "I'm sorry that I didn't even think about that before now."

"It's okay," she said. "I did think about it—and decided that

I preferred to spend our first Christmas together here, just the two of us."

"Just the two of us and my whole crazy family, you mean?"

"Well, yeah," she agreed. "But at least we'll have a few hours to ourselves Christmas morning."

And they made very good use of those few hours.

"Best Christmas ever," Winter said happily, naked and sated in her husband's arms.

"But only until next year," Luca noted, splaying his palm over the curve of her belly. "Next year will be even better because it will be our baby's first Christmas."

"And this baby is only the beginning," she promised. "The beginning of a long, happy life—and hopefully lots of babies—together."

"Lots, huh?" he said, nuzzling her throat. "Then maybe we better get some practice in."

She chuckled softly. "I think I can safely say that you don't need any more practice."

"Are you saying you don't want to practice?" he asked, nibbling her ear.

"I definitely didn't say that."

So they made love again, and afterward they ventured to the living room to open the presents under the tree.

For Luca, Winter had chosen a pair of leather work gloves that she'd seen him contemplating at Tenacity Feed and Seed (needed), a sports channel subscription (wanted) and *The Baby Owner's Manual* (to read). For Winter, Luca had followed through on his promise and bought a case of her body wash (needed), a handknit sweater that he'd caught her eyeing at the Christmas market (wanted) and a recent release by her favorite romance author (to read).

"There's one more present under the tree," Winter noted, after they'd each opened their three gifts.

"So there is," he said, reaching under the tree for the small square box.

"There aren't supposed to be any more presents."

"I'm aware of the rules," he said. "I don't know why you'd assume I'm responsible for this."

"You're saying you're not?" she challenged.

Instead of directly responding to her question, he read the tag affixed to the gift. "To Winter and Luca, From Santa."

"Santa, huh?"

"That's what it says," he confirmed, offering her the box.

She removed the bow and tag first, then tore off the paper. Inside the box, buried in layers of tissue, was a wooden disk etched with the silhouettes of a bride and a groom beneath a sprig of mistletoe, the beautifully detailed image framed by the words "Our First Christmas as Mr. & Mrs."

She lifted the ornament out of the box by the loop of twine punched through the hole at the top and turned it over to discover the back had been personalized with their names and wedding date.

"Luca, this is...perfect."

He peered at the ornament, as if seeing it for the first time.

"Gotta give Santa props for that one," he agreed.

She rolled her eyes even as she leaned forward to press a lingering kiss to his lips. "Well, you can add my thanks, too, the next time you're chatting with the big guy."

"I will," he promised, as she hung the ornament—front and center—on the tree.

"You know, this could be the start of a tradition for us," he told her. "Maybe Santa will bring us a new ornament to add to the tree every year—and eventually we'll be able to put the ones I painted in kindergarten back into storage."

"I love the idea of starting new traditions with you," she said with a smile. "But there's not a chance that I'm ever packing your childhood ornaments away."

* * *

"What time are we supposed to be at your parents' house?" Winter asked, after a leisurely shower during which they'd used a generous amount of her new body wash.

"Má said that dinner would be served at one."

She glanced at her watch. "We're going to be late," she said, as she hurriedly pulled Sera's red dress over her head.

"We're newlyweds," he reminded her. "No one expects us to be on time."

"Don't say that," she protested. "I don't want to think about your parents thinking about us doing…"

"What we were just doing?" he asked, finishing her sentence for her, his voice tinged with amusement.

"Exactly," she agreed.

"I don't think punctuality is going to stop the speculation—not when you've got beard burn on your throat and your lips are swollen from my kisses…and now your cheeks are as red as your dress."

"You like embarrassing me, don't you?"

"No," he denied. "But I like doing the things that make you blush when you think about them."

"Stop it. Right now," she demanded.

Luca just grinned.

There were some knowing glances exchanged when Luca and Winter finally showed up at his parents' house for the midday meal. And yes, she blushed to think that everyone else—or at least the adults present—might secretly be speculating about the reasons for their tardy arrival. Or, in the case of Stanley and Winona, discussing the matter outright.

"How is it that the couple who live closest is the last to arrive?" Uncle Stanley grumbled.

"They're newlyweds," his nonagenarian wife reminded him.

"Ah." Stanley gave an abrupt nod. "We know a little something about bronc riding in the bedroom rodeo, don't we?"

"Yee-haw," Winona said with a wink.

"On that note, I think I'll start putting dinner on the table," Nicole said.

"I'll help," Winter offered, hurrying to the kitchen after her mother-in-law.

A short while later, they were all seated at the table. Actually, it was two long tables that had been put together to accommodate the expanded Sanchez family, and before the platters of meat and bowls of vegetables were passed around, Will gave thanks for this opportunity to come together to celebrate the birth of Jesus and thank His Father for the countless blessings He'd bestowed upon their family, including all the new members who had increased their number this year.

Beneath the table, Luca squeezed Winter's hand, and she sent up her own silent prayer of thanks for Luca, the family he'd made her part of and the life they were making together.

Chapter Fifteen

Winter had quickly learned that there was always work to be done on a cattle ranch, and though Luca hadn't had to work on Christmas, he was up and gone early the next day. But she had no cause for complaint, as he usually hurried to finish whatever tasks were required of him so that he could return home as soon as possible. Occasionally he was early enough to help her with dinner preparations, and though she protested that he should take some time to relax after putting in a full day, he was happier to be in the kitchen with her—sometimes helping, sometimes hindering, but always affectionate and tender.

On the third day after Christmas, Winter had contemplated going into town to put in a few hours at Castillo's, but Luca suggested she hold off as a snowstorm was expected later in the day. He didn't tell her not to go. As always, he let the choice be hers—sharing his thoughts but giving her credit for being able to make her own decisions.

So she stayed home, because she had no desire to battle the weather. Also, she was halfway through the book he'd given her for Christmas and eager to finish it. (Now that she wasn't going to bed alone at night, she didn't have nearly as much time to read as she'd had in the first days of her marriage, and she wasn't the least bit unhappy about it.)

She was just about to take her book and a cup of herbal tea into the living room when her phone rang. A quick glance at the display had her smiling as she connected the call.

"Alice, it's so good to hear from you," she said to her friend and former neighbor in Butte.

"You've been on my mind so much the past few weeks," Alice told her. "Getting ready for Christmas, I found myself thinking of everything we did together in recent years, shopping and wrapping presents and baking cookies. I should have called you before now to tell you I've been missing you."

"I've missed you, too," Winter said, though the truth was, she'd had so much fun with Luca's family and Rafael and Sera this year, she hadn't spared more than a thought for her friend. "But the holidays are always a busy time, and I'm glad you're reaching out now."

"How was your Christmas?" Alice asked.

"It was wonderful." This time, her response was completely sincere. "And yours?"

Her friend sighed. "Pretty close to disastrous."

"Oh, no. What happened?"

"My parents decided to go to Fiji for the holidays, my sister went to Jamaica—not the island but the town in Iowa—with her fiancé and Kyle moved out three weeks ago."

"I'm so sorry."

"That's not the worst of it," Alice confided.

"I'm listening," Winter assured her.

"I was alone and lonely and so, when Matt suggested that, rather than each of us being alone, we should hang out together, I decided—why not?"

"So you spent Christmas with Matt," she noted cautiously.

"Christmas Day…and Christmas night."

Winter fell silent.

"I'm so sorry," Alice said.

"You don't have to apologize for sleeping with my ex-husband," she told her friend. "Our divorce was final months ago."

"You're really not mad?"

"I'm really not mad," she promised.

Alice exhaled an audible sigh of relief. "I was so afraid you were going to hate me. But he's so handsome and charming and...well, I was probably a little drunk... But it was only once. In the morning, we were both awkward and embarrassed, agreed it was a mistake and would never happen again. And it won't. I swear."

"You don't have to make any promises to me, either," Winter said. "But now I feel like I should apologize to you."

"Because you never told me he was selfish and self-centered in bed?" her friend quipped.

"In my defense, I didn't actually know he was selfish and self-centered in bed."

It took Alice a minute to understand what Winter was saying.

"He was your first?" her friend asked, stunned.

"Yeah."

"Well, hopefully you'll meet someone new and wonderful who can expand your horizons."

Winter could feel the smile spread across her face. "Horizons expanded."

"Good for you," Alice said, sounding sincerely pleased now.

"There's something else you want to say," Winter realized.

"While I was hanging out with Matt on Christmas, he told me that he knew you'd lied about being in California. I pretended to be surprised, but I think he knew I was lying, too. Then he said he'd been in touch with your parents, and your mom told him that you'd been staying with a cousin in Tenacity."

Winter already knew her mom had outed her location to Matt, because she'd confronted her after receiving the wedding photo he'd sent. And though she was frustrated that Josefina hadn't honored her request to not talk to her ex-husband about her, she knew better than anyone how persuasive he could be when he wanted something.

"I appreciate you letting me know," she said to Alice.

"That's not all," her friend confided. "I saw him with a duffle bag over his shoulder this morning and asked if he was going on vacation. He said he was just taking a quick trip to get back something he'd lost. Then he gave me a strange half smile and said, 'Two things, actually. Or maybe just one and a half.'"

Winter suddenly felt cold all over.

Cold and shaky and sick.

But she swallowed the bile that had risen in her throat and managed to reply, "That's an odd statement to make."

"Exactly what I thought," Alice agreed. "And maybe I'm way off base, but there was something about his tone that made me think he's on his way to Tenacity to find you."

Winter was visibly trembling when she disconnected the call—so much so that it took her three attempts to hit the right button on the screen.

It was her own fault.

She'd let her guard down.

Over the past few weeks, she'd been so focused on her new life with Luca that she'd let her concerns about Matt fade into the background. She'd chosen to enjoy being married to an amazing man who treated her with care and respect—and introduced her to pleasures she'd been certain didn't exist outside the pages of her favorite romance novels—rather than spare a thought to her ex-husband. Because, for the first time in a long time, she felt truly happy and excited about her future.

Even when Matt had sent the wedding photo and, later, that ridiculous display of roses, she hadn't completely freaked out because she knew he'd been playing mind games from a distance.

But if he was on his way to Tenacity...

Two things, actually. Or maybe just one and a half.

His cryptic remark to Alice had to have been a reference to her pregnancy—but how could he know?

She rubbed gentle circles on her belly, hoping that the stress she was feeling wouldn't be transmitted to the baby in her womb.

"Nothing but happy thoughts," she said in a singsong voice, as she desperately tried to conjure such thoughts. "Unicorns and rainbows. Sparkly unicorns prancing over kaleidoscopic rainbows."

But her mind continued to churn.

If Matt came to Tenacity...if he managed to track her here, to the home she shared with Luca...

He would ruin everything.

Just by showing up, he'd spoil the happiness she'd found here.

And she couldn't let that happen.

"Tail-wagging puppies. Giggling babies." She continued to rub her belly. "Babies giggling at tail-wagging puppies."

She couldn't just sit around and wait—she had to do something.

But what?

She didn't know. She couldn't think.

Do you even have a brain in that head of yours?

She pushed the echo of his voice out of her mind and hurried to the bedroom, retrieving a suitcase from the back of the closet. She opened it on the bed and started filling it, transferring the contents of her drawers into the case, until it could hold no more, then she zipped it up and dragged it to the door.

I have to leave Tenacity. I have to go somewhere that Matt will never find me—so he can never find my baby.

She lifted her coat off the hook and shoved her arms into the sleeves at the same time she stuffed her feet into her boots. Then she dropped her cell phone into the side pocket of her purse and, with her suitcase in one hand and keys in the other, opened the door.

The blast of cold air stole her breath as snow swirled around her.

Somehow, in the brief amount of time that had passed since

Alice's call, she'd completely forgotten Luca's concerns about the forecast—that information having been pushed out of her mind by the enormity of the revelation that Matt was on his way to Tenacity.

Significant snowfall was always a complication for cattle ranchers—but never a surprise in winter in Montana. And although the weather gave Winter pause, a little snow—or even a blizzard—was unlikely to alter Matt's plans, and so she couldn't let it alter hers, either.

It was only after she'd stowed her suitcase in the back of her SUV and was driving away from the cabin that she acknowledged she didn't have a plan—only panic.

But that panic was enough to keep her foot on the accelerator.

Luca was glad when the ranch foreman told him to go home early. Not because he was particularly concerned about the snow that had started to come down fast and thick, but because he was eager to get home to his wife.

He'd just sent a text to let her know he was on his way when his phone rang. He answered with a smile on his face, assuming she was calling in response to his message.

"¡Hola! Cariño."

There was a pause on the other end before a male voice responded, "I appreciate the term of affection, *primo*, but I have a wife who holds my heart."

Rafael.

"Obviously I didn't realize it was *you* calling," Luca pointed out to his wife's cousin.

"You should check call display before you embarrass yourself," Rafael advised. "Oops—too late."

"Funny."

"All kidding aside," the other man said, his tone serious now. "I'm calling to tell you that Matt Hathaway's in town."

"Hijo de puta."

"Yeah, that just about sums it up," Rafael agreed.

"What's he doing here?"

"Exactly what I asked, when he walked in and sat down at the bar. He claimed he only wanted a drink, so I poured him a beer and he started chatting up Howard Prescott," the bartender said, naming a local resident who was something of a fixture at Castillo's.

"At first they seemed to be having an animated discussion about the 49ers, so I tuned them out and went about my business, but then I heard Matt mention Winter's name, asking Howard if he knew her and if he'd seen her around.

"I shut down his questions quick," Rafael assured Luca. "But he asserted that he had a right to know where his wife was."

"*Ex*-wife," Luca ground out between clenched teeth.

"I made that point, too," the other man said. "And Howard immediately clammed up, paid for his drink and walked out."

"And Matt?"

"He hung around for a second beer—more, I think, because he knew I wanted him gone than because he wanted to stay. Anyway, he left about five minutes ago. I have no idea where he was heading next or what his intentions are, but I wanted to give you a heads-up."

"I appreciate it," Luca said.

"I tried calling Winter, too, but I got her voicemail."

"I'm on my way home now. I'll give her the update when I get there."

But when he disconnected from Rafael, he decided to try calling Winter himself. His call went straight to voicemail, too.

Winter's knuckles were white on the steering wheel as she drove through the storm. But while her gaze was fixed on the snow-covered road, her mind wandered.

Now that she had some distance from Matt and her marriage to him, she could appreciate that he was nothing more than a bully. Yes, he was bigger and stronger than her, and physically, she was no match for him. But he'd never wielded that superior physical strength in front of other people, because he didn't want others to know that he was a bully who berated and pushed around his wife.

But she wasn't his wife anymore.

She was married to Luca now. She had a husband who'd shown her what it was like to love and be loved. Even if he'd never said the words, she knew he cared about her. Deeply. And maybe, in the future, that caring would turn to love.

But if she ran away now, she'd have no future with Luca.

If she ran away now, Matt would win.

She wasn't going to let him win.

But the snow was falling fast and thick now—big fat flakes that splatted against her windshield, obscuring her vision. She increased the speed of the wiper blades, but the snow was still coming faster than she could clear it. Not the kind of weather she really wanted to be driving in—even if the only place she wanted to go now was home.

Cautiously, carefully, she eased her SUV to the side of the road and put on her hazard lights, intending to stay put until the worst of the storm had passed.

She was pretty sure Luca had said the snow would be done by four. The clock on the dash read 3:28.

Or did he say six?

Or did he say they were expecting four to six inches?

Obviously she should have listened more closely.

Is it too much of a challenge for you to pay attention for two goddamn minutes?

She shook her head, as if that might banish the memory of Matt's hurtful words. He'd spent the better part of four years undermining her belief in herself, making her feel worthless and useless and stupid.

But she'd been smart enough to get away from him, and she wasn't going to let those distant echoes undermine her now.

Luca's phone was ringing again when he pulled into his driveway.

This time, he checked the caller ID before answering—and frowned when he saw the Grizzly Bar on the display.

"Hello?" Luca said, certain it was a misdial.

"Hey, Luke. It's Cameron."

"What's up, Cameron?" he asked, trying not to sound impatient because the only person he wanted to hear from was the one person who hadn't called.

"I'm not sure," his friend said. "Maybe it's nothing, but there's a guy sitting at the bar—an out-of-towner, I'd guess, or at least nobody I've ever seen before—asking questions about Winter Hathaway. I'm not sure I've heard the name 'Hathaway' before, but 'Winter' isn't a very common name so I wondered if he might be asking about your wife."

"I'd guess *yes* and that it's her ex-husband," Luca said grimly.

"I didn't realize she'd been married before."

"It's ancient history."

"Maybe someone should tell her ex-husband that," Cameron said. "Because he's not talking about her as if she's in the past."

"I'll tell him," Luca promised. "I'll make it very clear to him."

"He's gone," Cameron said without preamble when Luca walked into the bar forty minutes later, after a quick stop at home.

"When?"

"Just left. You might have passed him driving out of the parking lot as you were driving in."

"*Maldito.*" Luca scrubbed his hands over his face. "What else can you tell me?"

"He demanded a third whiskey and when I refused to serve him, he got nasty. Threatened me and everyone else in the bar and—" Cameron eyed him warily "—I'm not sure if I should tell you this, but he had some pretty harsh words for Winter, too. Said he was going to find his wife without any help from us stupid hicks and remind her where she belonged.

"No one here said a word about his ex-wife now being your wife," the bartender hastened to assure him. "But you know how some people like to talk, so he might have better luck at his next stop."

"Always a possibility," Luca acknowledged.

"You take care of that pretty bride," Cameron said.

"Will do," he promised.

But first he needed to find her.

Chapter Sixteen

What had she been thinking?

Winter sighed as she watched the snow swirl around her vehicle.

The problem, most likely, was that she hadn't been thinking. That, after her conversation with Alice, she'd panicked and, desperate to ensure that Matt wouldn't be able to find her, left the only place she'd felt safe in months—her home with Luca.

Now she was out in the middle of a storm, definitely not feeling safe, wanting only to be in the warm comfort of her husband's arms.

You're a smart, strong, amazing woman.

The echo of Luca's words in the back of her mind made her smile—and inspired her to be the woman he believed her to be.

Because wanting to be with him didn't mean that she needed a man to take care of her, and enjoying his comfort and companionship wasn't evidence that she was too weak to survive on her own. On the contrary, it was proof that she was strong enough to open her heart again and smart enough to trust where it led her.

The last time she was at a loss to know what to do—the day she'd taken the pregnancy test—she'd turned to Luca. For reasons she still didn't fully understand, she'd instinctively trusted him to come through for her. And he'd done so.

So why, when she'd found herself at a loss again, had she turned away from him?

Though he'd only been her husband for a few short weeks,

the one thing she knew for certain, without a shadow of a doubt, was that she loved him. And even if Luca didn't love her the same way, she knew that he had feelings for her. She knew that he cared about her and their baby and that he would do anything in his power to protect both of them.

So even if Matt was in Tenacity, looking for her, what's the worst that he could do? They were no longer married; he had no authority over her. Not that he had any while they were married, either, even if he'd liked to assert otherwise. More important, she wasn't alone anymore. She had Luca by her side, and she trusted that he would always be there.

Admittedly it made her a little uneasy to think that Matt might ask questions about the baby and possibly cause people to wonder if the child she carried could be his. But she would stand in the middle of the town square, if necessary, and yell at the top of her lungs, without any compunction, that Luca Sanchez was the father of her baby. Because in her heart and soul, it was one hundred percent true.

Squinting through the windshield now, it seemed to Winter as if the snow was letting up a little. Yeah, it was still blowing, but it wasn't coming down as fast or as thick.

Most of the residents of Tenacity were apparently smarter than she was, because there wasn't any traffic on the road. In fact, she hadn't seen another vehicle pass, in either direction, since she'd pulled over.

So maybe, as long as she took her time, she could go home.

She touched a hand to the slight swell of her belly and felt... something.

A kick?

Or just a flutter of anxiety?

She was in her nineteenth week now and the doctor had suggested she might be able to feel movement—described by some expectant moms as flutters or pulses—around week twenty. So while it might be a little early to feel the baby moving, maybe her *chiquita*—or *chiquito*—knew that mama needed to know that she wasn't alone right now.

"I'm sorry, *bebé*. Your mamá's been stressing out today and made some impulsive and unwise decisions. But my head's clearer now and I'm going to take you home. As soon as we're back home with your papá, everything's going to be okay. *Yo prometo*."

Checking her mirrors to ensure there still weren't any other vehicles around, Winter shifted into Drive and slowly inched forward, pulling sharply on the steering wheel to make a U-turn.

Several inches of snow had accumulated on the road, and her tires spun a little.

She could tell her front passenger side had dropped off the edge of the roadway, onto the soft shoulder. So she pressed a little harder on the accelerator, to give her SUV the power to climb onto the hard surface again. Unfortunately her tire bumped up the curb, hit on a patch of ice and immediately starting sliding again, this time sending the back end of the vehicle sliding, too, in the opposite direction.

Steer into the skid.

She did so intuitively, but perhaps she tugged too hard on the wheel—or maybe she forgot to take her foot off the pedal. Whatever the cause, the effect was that her SUV continued to slide until it was nose-first in the shallow ditch that ran parallel to the road.

Winter dropped her head to the steering wheel and cursed in frustration, then immediately apologized to her baby again.

Obviously she was going to have to call for a tow truck to get her out of the ditch, but first she needed to call Luca, to let him know where she was and that she was okay.

Stuck, but okay.

Her hands were shaking as she reached into her purse for her cell phone, and she found herself wishing that she'd ignored Alice's call earlier in the day. If she'd done so, she might still be at home, snuggling under a warm throw, reading the last pages of her book.

She swiped to open the screen and discovered that she'd missed several calls from Luca. In addition, he'd sent a series of text messages.

Boss is letting everyone go home early. See you soon. XO

Home now. Where R U?

Looks like a tornado tore through the bedroom—what's going on?

Really starting to worry here.

PLS CALL ME

She immediately tapped his name to initiate a call.

"Winter. *Gracias a Dios.*"

"I'm so sorry," she said. "The ringer was turned off on my phone and I didn't get any of your messages until right now."

"It's okay," he said. "I'm just so relieved to hear your voice."

"Me, too."

"Where are you?"

"Second Street. Not too far past the intersection of Second and Grant. More specifically, in a ditch on Second Street not too far past the intersection with Grant."

"*Dios, cariño*—are you okay?"

"I'm fine. I promise. I actually pulled over to the side of the road to wait out the storm then, when the snow began to let up, I tried to turn my vehicle around to come home and slid off the road."

She heard him curse under his breath. "You're sure you're okay?"

"It was a slow slide," she told him. "My airbag didn't even deploy."

"But why were you out? Where were you going?"

"A momentary brain lapse," she said, not wanting to tell him about Alice's call over the phone. "But it's all good now."

"I'll be there in fifteen minutes," he promised.

"No," she protested. "I don't want to worry about you on the roads in this weather."

"My vehicle can handle it better than yours," he assured her.

"Okay," she relented. "But be careful."

"Always," he promised.

The snow had lessened up, Luca noted with some relief, as he left the Grizzly and headed toward Second Street.

Of course, the greatest source of relief was having heard Winter's voice and knowing that she was safe.

It was hard to believe only a couple hours had passed since that first phone call from Rafael, telling him that Matt Hathaway was in town. He felt as if he'd lived days—maybe even weeks—in that span, not knowing where his wife was or if her ex-husband had made any progress in his efforts to find her.

For the past few weeks, Luca had been reluctant to put a label on his feelings, especially when it seemed that there were more important things going on in their marriage than his growing affection for his bride. Then he'd gone home and discovered she was gone—along with a suitcase and half her clothes—and the possibility that he might lose her had been like a dagger to his heart.

He had questions about the suitcase, about where she'd planned to go, but those questions could wait. Or maybe, since she'd been on her way home when her car went off the road, they didn't even need to be asked.

In less than the fifteen minutes he'd estimated, he arrived at

Second Street. As he made his way toward the intersection at Grant, he saw the flashing lights of emergency vehicles.

Apprehension knotted in his belly as he inched closer to the police blockade.

An officer, wearing a bright orange vest over his uniform, his shoulders hunched against the bitter wind, approached the driver's side of Luca's vehicle.

He lowered the window just far enough to make conversation possible.

"Road's closed, sir. You have to turn around."

Beyond the blockade, he could see that a pickup truck had decided to challenge a lamppost—and lost the battle in spectacular fashion.

"I need to get to my wife," Luca said. "Her vehicle slid into the ditch across the road."

"Then she's luckier than this guy," the officer—"Paul" according to the badge on his jacket—told him. "And she'll have to wait while you go the long way around."

Luca couldn't look away from the wreckage. There was an ambulance at the ready, waiting for the fire department to pry open the door of the truck and free the occupant.

The knots in his stomach tightened.

"The vehicle doesn't look familiar," he remarked, his tone casual and conversational. "Is the driver local?"

The officer shook his head. "From Butte, according to the address on his license."

Luca swallowed. "Matt Hathaway?"

Officer Paul's gaze narrowed. "You know him?"

"I met him once."

So it *was* Winter's ex-husband in that truck.

And Winter was just on the other side of the intersection.

Icy fingers of fear scraped down his spine.

What if Matt had found Winter's stranded vehicle before running into that lamppost?

He shifted into Park, right there in the middle of the road.

"Sir," Officer Paul said again, obviously losing patience when Luca pushed open his door and climbed out of his truck. "You can't park here."

"My wife…" Those were the only words he managed to push past the constriction in his throat.

Another vehicle pulled up behind Luca then, and the officer moved past him, no doubt to direct the second driver to turn around. Luca took advantage of his preoccupation to push forward, determined to make his way through the first responders gathered around the wreck to the opposite side of the cross-street, where Winter was stranded. Because he refused to believe that God could be so cruel as to take her away when he'd only just realized how much he loved her and wanted to spend the rest of his life—hopefully a very long time—with her.

"Luca!"

He paused in mid-step, wondering if he'd actually heard her calling his name or just imagined it.

"Luca!"

Definitely not his imagination.

He pivoted in the snow, and there she was.

Winter.

His shaky legs were suddenly steady again, allowing him to race toward her, gather her in his arms and hug her tight. He drew back briefly to examine her, his hands running over her, checking for bumps and bruises—as if he might find anything through the puffy coat she wore—before pulling her close again.

"I'm fine, Luca," she told him, her words muffled against his coat.

He exhaled a sigh of relief. "You're fine. Safe."

Mine.

"You were supposed to stay in your car," he reminded her.

"A police car en route to the accident saw my SUV on the side of the road and stopped. The driver turned out to be Officer Karlsson. I told him that I was waiting for you, but he didn't think it was safe for me to stay there so he brought me here instead—insisting, of course, that I wait in his cruiser so that he didn't have to worry about a civilian wandering around an accident scene. But when I saw your vehicle, he agreed that I could meet you—as long as I promised to stay out of the way.

"I called a tow truck while I was waiting," she continued. "But it turns out more than a few vehicles ended up in ditches because of the storm, so mine might be stuck until tomorrow."

She glanced at the truck mangled against the lamppost then and shivered. "I'm glad I pulled over when I did. I realize my situation could have been a lot worse if I'd continued to drive through the storm."

"You would have had to be going really fast to lose control like that," Luca remarked, sliding his arm across her shoulders to steer her toward his vehicle and away from the accident scene.

After a few steps, Winter paused. "That looks like... Matt's truck."

Luca debated with himself for half a minute before he confirmed, "It is Matt's truck."

Winter looked up at him, eyes wide.

"One of the officers at the blockade shared the identity of the driver."

"Oh." Now she took a minute to consider this revelation. "A friend from Butte called earlier to tell me she thought Matt was coming to Tenacity. I hoped she was wrong."

"She wasn't."

Winter nodded slowly.

"Officer Paul indicated that he's in pretty rough shape."

She swallowed. "How bad?"

"I don't know. And, to be honest, I didn't think to ask. My only concern was for you."

"I'm sorry."

"There's no reason for you to apologize."

"I shouldn't have left the cabin," she said now. "But after talking to Alice... I panicked."

"It's okay, *cariño*."

"It's not," she said, sniffling a little. "Running away was a knee-jerk reaction based on fear. For most of the time I was married to Matt, I was afraid of him. But as I drove away from the cabin, I realized I wasn't afraid of him anymore. My biggest fear was never seeing you again. Never having the chance to tell you how much I love you. Because I do, Luca. I love you with everything in my heart and my soul."

He framed her face in his gloved hands, so that she could see the truth and depth of his feelings in his eyes when he responded to her declaration with his own. "And I love you, Winter. My beautiful, smart, sexy, strong, amazing wife. You are the piece of my life that I didn't even know was missing until you came back to Tenacity. You are my heart and my soul. My everything. *Para siempre*."

Then he lowered his head and kissed her, right there in the middle of the street, with emergency lights flashing all around them. And she kissed him back, mindless of the snow falling and the wind blowing, aware only that her heart was full to overflowing.

"Are you ready to go home now?" Luca asked, when he finally lifted his mouth from hers. "Or do you want to see if we can get some information about Matt?"

"I'm more than ready to go home," Winter said. "But can we check his status? As much as I want him out of my life forever, I'd never wish him dead."

"Let's find Karlsson," he suggested.

So that's what they did, and after Winter identified herself as Matt Hathaway's ex-wife, the officer gave her a quick update.

"Serious but not life-threatening injuries," Karlsson told them. "It could have been a lot worse—and it could have been prevented if he hadn't been drunk behind the wheel."

"You must be relieved that he's going to be okay," Luca said, as he and Winter finally made their way back to his truck—still parked in the middle of the road on the other side of the blockade.

She nodded. "Relieved—and anxious. Because I know he came to Tenacity for me. And I don't know what he knows or thinks he knows about my life now, but I know that I need to see him, to finally put the past behind me. Behind *us*. So that we can move forward with our future together."

"If you insist on seeing him, then I'm going with you."

"I appreciate that you're looking out for me, but I need to confront him on my own—to prove to myself that I'm strong and capable enough to do so."

"You shouldn't ever doubt how strong and capable you are," Luca said, reaching across the console to take her hand. "And I need to go with you, so that you know you're not alone. Not ever again."

Matt Hathaway was being arraigned when they arrived at the hospital the next day, so that he could be transferred to the local lockup as soon as the doctors released him from the hospital.

He had a concussion, a couple of cracked ribs, a ruptured spleen, sprained wrist, a broken nose and two black eyes—the latter injuries caused by the force of the airbag deployment, without which he likely would not have survived the crash.

He was being charged with driving in excess of the posted speed limit, failing to stop at a stop sign, driving under the influence, uttering threats—numerous counts as a result of numerous threats made at the Grizzly—and damage to public property.

"Doesn't look like you're going to be able to wriggle your way out of these charges," Winter noted, when the judge and attorneys had left the room. Luca had gone with her to the hospital, as promised, but agreed to wait outside the room, in accordance with her request.

"They want to throw the book at me just because I had a couple of drinks," he grumbled. "But I'll plead the charges down."

She wasn't surprised by his attitude. As always, he was looking for someone else to blame for the consequences of his own actions.

"You could have been killed," Winter felt compelled to point out.

"And leave you a widow? No way," he said.

She ignored the bait, saying instead, "Even worse, you might have killed an innocent bystander."

"But I didn't," he said dismissively.

"You're lucky you didn't."

"I always said you were my lucky charm."

"Except when you said I was holding you back and weighing you down."

He shrugged, then winced as the movement jarred his broken ribs.

"But that's all in the past," Winter said now.

"You here to talk about the future?"

"No. I'm here to tell you, clearly and concisely, that I don't ever want to see you again."

"And yet you're standing in my hospital room," he pointed out. "And how did you know I was here? Who told you I was in town?"

"Alice gave me a heads-up that you were looking for me."

"So she lied to me when she said she didn't know where you were."

"I asked her not to tell you," Winter admitted.

"A man has a right to know where his wife is."

"I'm not your wife," she reminded him.

"We exchanged vows."

"And you broke those vows. Every single one of them."

"I made some mistakes," he allowed. "But now that we're having a baby—"

"We're not having a baby," she interjected.

"Well, then, you need to go on a diet, honey, because you've put on some weight around the middle."

So much for thinking her sweater might disguise her baby bump.

"*I'm* having a baby," she said. "Me and Luca."

Matt scowled at that. "The guy you introduced me to when we came to Tenacity last year?"

She nodded.

"He's been sleeping with my wife?"

"No, he's been sleeping with *his* wife," she responded in an even tone.

"You got married again?" His gaze immediately went to her left hand, as if seeking confirmation. "When?"

"That's not any of your business."

"When's the baby due?"

"Also not any of your business," she said, pleased that her voice was steady and strong.

In the past, Matt had been able to make her cower with little more than a withering glance or a harsh word. And even if he was the same bully now that he'd always been, she wasn't the same woman and she wasn't going to let him bully her ever again.

"Then I guess I'll have to get the information from Dr. Carrington's office."

She must have shown some kind of reaction to his mention of the doctor's name, though, because a slow, smug smile spread across Matt's face.

"You really should keep your contact information up-to-date," he chided. "Because when your new ob-gyn contacted Dr. Mehta's office to request your medical records, Dr. Mehta's office reached out to ask where they should send the medical release to be signed. And when they couldn't get you on your cell, they left a message on our machine."

Winter steeled her spine and lifted her chin. "And now that those records have been released, you shouldn't be bothered by Dr. Mehta's office again."

"It wasn't a bother," he said. "It was…enlightening."

He had that predatory gleam in his eye, the one that she'd quickly learned to recognize and fear. But she wasn't afraid of him anymore.

"If you came to Tenacity because you were under the mistaken assumption that I was pregnant with your baby, you can go back to Butte—when you get out of prison, that is—knowing the truth, that Luca is my husband and the father of my child."

The predatory gleam morphed into a petulant scowl. "And if you think a jail cell is going to keep me away from you, let me assure you that the bars aren't necessary," he said, already putting his own spin on the story. "While I'm a little disappointed to discover that you've jumped so quickly into another marriage—and starting a family with your new husband—it's obvious that you've moved on and maybe now I can, too."

"I hope you do," Winter said.

"I did come to find you because I assumed, if you were pregnant, the baby was mine."

"It's not," she responded firmly, her gaze unwavering.

"Then I guess that's lucky for you," he finally said. "No doubt you think your new husband will be a better father to your baby than I could have been."

"No doubt he will be," she agreed.

And then she walked out the door.

"Are you okay?" Luca asked his wife, when they'd returned to their cabin after visiting the hospital.

"I am," Winter confirmed with a nod. "And even cautiously optimistic that Matt's ready to move on, too—when he gets out of jail."

"You're not feeling sorry for him, are you?"

She shook her head. "After everything he's done, it's where he should be."

"And how about you?" he asked. "Where do you want to be?"

"Right where I am." She drew his mouth to hers for a leisurely kiss. "With you."

"A lucky coincidence," he said. "Because with you is where I want to be. *Por ahora y siempre.*"

"For now and forever," she agreed.

Epilogue

Two weeks later

Winter studied the Silver Spur Café menu for a ridiculous amount of time, as if she'd never seen it before or perhaps couldn't decipher the language in which it was written.

"Can't decide between pancakes and waffles today?" Luca guessed.

"I definitely want waffles," she said. "But I'm wavering between bacon and sausage."

"So order both."

She shook her head regretfully. "I can't justify the extra calories."

"Isn't eating for two justification enough?"

He didn't bother to whisper the question. They'd told enough people about her pregnancy by now to feel confident that the news had made its way around town. A good thing, she acknowledged, as the bulky sweaters she favored wouldn't be able to hide her baby bump for much longer.

"You've been reading the same books I have, so you should know that being pregnant doesn't mean I can eat twice as much."

"What I know is that a man would have to be a fool to get between a pregnant woman and whatever she's craving."

She looked at him over the top of her menu, unamused.

He just grinned.

And, as always when her husband smiled at her, her heart

swelled inside her chest, full of happiness and gratitude and more love than she'd ever imagined a heart could hold.

"This is a serious dilemma," she told him.

"Here's an idea," he said. "You order the bacon and I'll order the sausage and then we can share both."

She gasped. "You want me to share my bacon?"

"Obviously I misspoke," he immediately replied. "What I meant to say is that I'd be happy to let you have one or two—or even all three—of my sausages."

Her attention shifted back to the laminated page in her hand. "Maybe I should get the meat lovers' omelet, with bacon *and* sausage *and* ham."

"I thought you wanted waffles."

She sighed. "I do want waffles."

He plucked the menu out of her hand.

"Hey," she protested.

He slid out of the booth and dropped a quick kiss on her lips before going to the counter to place their order.

Stanley and Winona were ahead of him in line, and while Luca and his great-uncle began to chat, the old man's even older wife made her way to the booth where Winter was seated.

"Look at you," Winona said, greeting Winter with a warm smile. "You are absolutely glowing."

"Thank you."

"Must be all that yee-hawing in the bedroom, am I right?" Winona teased, her wink as bold as her red coat.

Which, Winter suspected, was just about the color of her cheeks right now.

"It's lovely to see you again," she said, declining to answer the other woman's question.

Winona chuckled as she settled across from Winter, in the seat Luca had recently vacated. Then she leaned across the table and dropped her voice to a whisper. "Didn't I tell you there would be light beyond the shadows?"

"You did," Winter confirmed. And though she hadn't had a clue what the old woman had been referring to at the time, recent events had proven her insight to be true.

"Because I knew that you were strong enough to trust that he would protect and love you." Her ancient blue eyes dropped to Winter's middle. "Both of you."

"You're a scary woman, Winona."

That earned another chuckle.

"Hope you don't mind us crashing your breakfast date," Stanley said to Winter, sliding onto the bench seat beside his wife as Luca distributed the drinks he carried—three cups of coffee and a glass of apple juice.

"Of course not," she assured him.

"We come here almost every morning for a cup of joe," Stanley continued.

"Every morning that we're in Tenacity," Winona clarified.

He nodded. "When we're in Bronco, we go to Bean & Biscotti."

"Or Bronco Java and Juice."

"Options are more limited here," Luca noted.

"And yet, you've still got everything you need," Winona said.

Luca smiled at Winter. "And everything I ever wanted."

"Well, aren't you every bit as charming as your great-uncle?" Winona mused, as Eileen—one of the café's regular servers—brought their orders to the table.

Belgian waffles for Winter, French toast for Luca, fruit and yogurt for Winona—"unfortunately, I don't have the metabolism I had when I was eighty," she said with a wink—and a breakfast sandwich for Stanley.

Winter looked from her plate to her husband. "You got me bacon and sausage."

Luca shrugged. "I decided your parents' impending visit was justification for both."

"You think I'm going to need my strength to deal with my mother?" she guessed.

"A distinct possibility," he agreed.

But since Winter had confided in her parents about everything that happened the night of the storm and her subsequent confrontation with Matt, they seemed to have a better understanding of what she'd endured in her marriage to him. And they couldn't say enough to adequately express their appreciation for Luca or their happiness that she'd fallen in love with and was starting a family with a truly good man.

"Except that you'll be the one dealing with her, since the purpose of their visit is to get to know their son-in-law better," she pointed out now. Because that was what Josefina had told her daughter when she'd shared their plans.

"I'm happy to do my part," Luca said sincerely. "And crossing my fingers that they might, someday, forgive me for the shotgun wedding."

"All that came before will be forgiven the first time they meet their granddaughter," Winona assured the expectant parents.

Winter frowned. "We don't know if the baby's a boy or a girl."

The old woman seemed surprised by this statement—and perhaps even a little chagrined. Then she shrugged. "I could be wrong."

"Not likely," Stanley said.

Winter nibbled on a piece of bacon, considering.

"I hope you're not wrong," Luca told the self-proclaimed psychic. "Because I can't imagine anything more wonderful than having a little girl who looks just like her mama."

"And she will," Winona promised. "The next one will be a boy, though, and the spittin' image of his papa."

"Spoiler alert," Stanley said.

"The alert is supposed to come before the spoiler," Winter pointed out, wondering why she felt annoyed when she didn't really believe the old woman's predictions would come true. Did she?

"I could be wrong," Winona said again.

But Winter realized that she didn't want her to be wrong, because she couldn't imagine anything more wonderful than having a son who looked like Luca—except if he also inherited his dad's innate kindness and goodness. A man who showed her the truth and depth of his feelings in the little things he did for her every day. Such as ordering bacon and sausage with her breakfast so she wouldn't have to choose.

And since he'd only got sausage for himself, she transferred a slice of bacon from her plate to his now.

"*That* is true love," Stanley said, with an approving nod.

"I know it," Luca agreed, winking at her.

After breakfast was finished but before the two couples went their separate ways, Winona hugged Winter tightly. "Embrace your happy life," she urged. "You've earned it."

It was advice the new bride and expectant mom was happy to take.

* * * * *

Don't miss the next installment of the new continuity
Montana Mavericks: Behind Closed Doors

The Maverick's Do-Over
by Melissa Senate

On sale December 2025, wherever Harlequin books and ebooks are sold.

And look for the previous books in the series:

The Maverick's Dating Deal
by New York Times *bestselling author Christine Rimmer*

The Maverick's Forever Home
by USA TODAY *bestselling author Sasha Summers*

Lassoed by a Maverick
by Rochelle Alers

Snowed in with the Maverick
by Elle Douglas

Available now!

Get up to 4 Free Books!

We'll send you 2 free books from each series you try PLUS a free Mystery Gift.

FREE Value Over **$25**

Both the **Harlequin® Special Edition** and **Harlequin® Heartwarming™** series feature compelling novels filled with stories of love and strength where the bonds of friendship, family and community unite.

YES! Please send me 2 FREE novels from the Harlequin Special Edition or Harlequin Heartwarming series and my FREE Gift (gift is worth about $10 retail). After receiving them, if I don't wish to receive any more books, I can return the shipping statement marked "cancel." If I don't cancel, I will receive 6 brand-new Harlequin Special Edition books every month and be billed just $6.39 each in the U.S. or $7.19 each in Canada, or 4 brand-new Harlequin Heartwarming Larger-Print books every month and be billed just $7.19 each in the U.S. or $7.99 each in Canada, a savings of 20% off the cover price. It's quite a bargain! Shipping and handling is just 50¢ per book in the U.S. and $1.25 per book in Canada.* I understand that accepting the 2 free books and gift places me under no obligation to buy anything. I can always return a shipment and cancel at any time by calling the number below. The free books and gift are mine to keep no matter what I decide.

Choose one:
- ☐ **Harlequin Special Edition** (235/335 BPA G36Y)
- ☐ **Harlequin Heartwarming Larger-Print** (161/361 BPA G36Y)
- ☐ **Or Try Both!** (235/335 & 161/361 BPA G36Z)

Name (please print)

Address   Apt. #

City   State/Province   Zip/Postal Code

Email: Please check this box ☐ if you would like to receive newsletters and promotional emails from Harlequin Enterprises ULC and its affiliates. You can unsubscribe anytime.

Mail to the Harlequin Reader Service:
IN U.S.A.: P.O. Box 1341, Buffalo, NY 14240-8531
IN CANADA: P.O. Box 603, Fort Erie, Ontario L2A 5X3

Want to explore our other series or interested in ebooks? Visit www.ReaderService.com or call 1-800-873-8635.

---

*Terms and prices subject to change without notice. Prices do not include sales taxes, which will be charged (if applicable) based on your state or country of residence. Canadian residents will be charged applicable taxes. Offer not valid in Quebec. This offer is limited to one order per household. Books received may not be as shown. Not valid for current subscribers to the Harlequin Special Edition or Harlequin Heartwarming series. All orders subject to approval. Credit or debit balances in a customer's account(s) may be offset by any outstanding balance owed by or to the customer. Please allow 4 to 6 weeks for delivery. Offer available while quantities last.

Your Privacy—Your information is being collected by Harlequin Enterprises ULC, operating as Harlequin Reader Service. For a complete summary of the information we collect, how we use this information and to whom it is disclosed, please visit our privacy notice located at https://corporate.harlequin.com/privacy-notice. Notice to California Residents – Under California law, you have specific rights to control and access your data. For more information on these rights and how to exercise them, visit https://corporate.harlequin.com/california-privacy. For additional information for residents of other U.S. states that provide their residents with certain rights with respect to personal data, visit https://corporate.harlequin.com/other-state-residents-privacy-rights/.

HSEHW25